Beside the Rolling Waves

RASPBERRY RIDGE
BOOK SEVEN

JESSIE GUSSMAN

Contents

Acknowledgments

Cover art by Julia Gussman
Editing by Heather Hayden
Narration by Jay Dyess
Author Services by CE Author Assistant

Listen to the unabridged audio for FREE performed by Jay Dyess on the Say with Jay channel on YouTube. Get early access to all of Jay's recordings and listen to Jessie's books before they're available to the general public, plus get daily Bible readings by Jay and bonus scenes by becoming a Say with Jay channel member.

One

Becky Peck opened a bleary eye and lifted one tentative hand out of the warm cocoon of her covers, slapping around on her almost freezing nightstand, trying to find her phone to shut off the alarm.

Finally, her groping fingers hit the snooze button, and she yanked her hand from the chilly air back underneath her cozy blankets. She had at least seven on her bed. And she wore a set of long underwear, two T-shirts, a long-sleeve T-shirt, a sweatshirt, and a puffer vest on the top, plus three or four layers on the bottom, along with a thin pair of socks underneath two warm wool pairs.

Her toes were still cold.

That probably meant her blankets had shifted during the night, but instead of trying to fix the blankets, she just pulled herself into a ball and used one of her hands to try to warm up her toes while closing her eyes and enjoying a couple more minutes of blessed rest.

Her day was going to be busy from the time her feet hit the floor until she fell into bed tonight. And she really should get out of bed and get it started.

But she dreaded the cold.

Her small apartment above the horse stable where she kept her precious babies was heated, but she kept the heat down to the very lowest it would go, just warm enough to keep the water lines from freezing. She couldn't afford the heat bill, not with the feed bill she had, plus the rent for the stable, and she did try to buy food for herself with whatever was left.

She ought to have health insurance, but she couldn't even think about that.

She wiggled around, trying to get the toes on her other foot where she could reach them. She moved so much, she knew she wasn't going back to sleep. So she might as well get up.

Bracing herself for the cold, dreading it, and wishing, just once, she could turn the heat up as high as she wanted, she took a deep breath and then threw the covers off, throwing her feet out of bed and going quickly to the bathroom.

It didn't take long at all to get dressed in her work clothes and pour a steaming hot cup of coffee.

She didn't really like coffee, and she had never needed it to wake up, but the warmth was what she craved, and she'd gotten herself hooked on the caffeine in the process. Not that it mattered.

Sometimes she wondered if anything mattered.

She'd always wanted to be around horses, it was her dream, but...she was sinking further and further into debt, and she had absolutely nothing to show for it.

Last summer, she hadn't made enough money on the carriage rides she gave tourists to even pay for the feed bill, let alone the farrier and vet bills, and the idea that she might eventually need another horse could cause her heart to stop for a couple of seconds. It certainly wasn't enough to support her. She did that by cleaning houses. But she only had so much time that she wasn't taking care of her horses, especially in the winter when ice needed to be broken, water hauled, snow scraped, and horses manually exercised, because she didn't want to chance them slipping on ice in the pasture. They were too expensive, too valuable, and she loved them too much for that. A horse with a broken leg would have to be put down.

She wrapped her hands around her coffee mug, eyeing her gloves by the door. She already had her coat on and her boots as well. The last thing to do was put her gloves on, pull her hat down over her ears, and head outside into the Michigan winter.

At least she didn't have to walk far to get to work, she thought to herself, not for the first time. She lived above the horse stable where her horses were stalled, so it smelled interesting in her apartment, but that didn't bother her, and her commute to work was her favorite part of her job.

No. Her favorite part of her job was the horses.

Draining the last of her coffee, she set the mug down on the counter to deal with later, grabbed her gloves, stuck them on, and then walked out the door.

Immediately the scent of horses and fresh manure hit her, and she breathed deeply. It smelled like home to her. Like safety and happiness and all the good things. That's part of the reason why she did what she did. Because she loved it. She loved this. Stepping out into a new day, breathing deeply of the smells that made her heart soar, and knowing that she got to do what so many people just dreamed of.

Sure, she lived below the poverty level, at a level that most people could not even begin to think of surviving at, and common luxuries, like toilet paper, were closely rationed, but...she loved her life.

There was only one thing missing.

"Good morning, Jasper," she said, walking down the stairs and petting the nose that stuck out of the stall.

Jasper was always up and waiting on her in the morning.

Sometimes Jethro, and the two mares, Velvet and Clementine, slept in a bit, but Jasper faced the day eagerly. He was always the one who wanted out, wanted to run, wanted to enjoy each new day, like it was a gift. He reminded her what a gift life really was. Sometimes she needed that reminder more than others.

"I wish I was as unaffected by the cold as you are," she said to Jasper as she scratched his wide forehead. Clydesdales were tall, a heavy draft breed. They were also extremely expensive, and that was part of what made her bills so high. She'd overextended herself buying all four of them.

She couldn't ask her adoptive parents, who would have insisted on giving her money and not allowed her to pay them back. Matt and

Jubilee Landry from Strawberry Sands had loaned her the money, and she knew that if she went to them and said she couldn't pay them back, they would be perfectly fine with it. They could afford to lose the money anyway. But there was something inside of her that absolutely would not allow her to not do what she said she was going to do. And when she asked to borrow the money, she told him she would pay a certain amount every month until it was paid back with interest.

It wasn't right to not keep her word. Because a man was only as good as his word. That went for women too.

She thought about someone who had not kept his word to her, and her heart broke a little, as it did every time she thought about Rodney.

But life went on, and she hadn't heard from him for a long time. And she wasn't going to worry about it. She was going to move on with her life.

She pushed her shoulders back and finished petting Jasper's wide forehead before she grabbed the bucket out of the gelding's stall, and another one out of Jethro's stall, and took them to the water hydrant at the front of the barn.

Hopefully it wasn't frozen this morning.

She saw the heat tape glowing and took that as a good sign.

Hooking the handle of the bucket over the back of the hydrant, she carefully turned it on so it didn't blast with full force at the bottom of the bucket, soaking her face and coat. She'd done that plenty of times and had done the rest of the morning chores with a frozen coat and frozen body. Getting her face flushed with cold water first thing on a subzero-temperature day served to wake a person up, that was for sure. But it also was exceptionally uncomfortable.

As the water filled the bucket, she grabbed her phone out.

Good morning, beautiful.

She smiled. It was Rick, her almost boyfriend.

She didn't take her gloves off to message him back, just used her nose to pull up the emojis and sent him a smiley face.

Rick would know she was working and understand.

Shoving her phone back in her pocket, she shut the water off, switched the buckets, and carefully turned the water back on. Then, while the second bucket was filling, she carried Jasper's bucket to him and opened the stall door, setting it down so he could drink his fill.

She'd go and fill it back up, and that time, she'd hook it into his stall.

The heat from the horse usually kept the water from freezing, but not always. It depended on the wind coming off of Lake Michigan and how low the temperatures dropped.

Grabbing a bucket from Velvet's stall, she hurried back, knowing from doing it over and over again that if she hurried, she could get there just as the bucket got full.

She timed it perfectly, shut the water off, hooked Velvet's bucket onto the water spout, turned it on, and hurried back to Jethro's stall.

It took a good fifteen minutes to completely water the horses, and then it was time to feed them.

Once they were fed, she would muck out their stalls, and then she would work on taking them out and giving them some exercise.

It wasn't strictly necessary, but she wanted them to be in good shape if she got a request for a carriage ride. Which, now that Christmas was over, bookings had slowed down to a trickle. Or maybe it had stopped altogether. She scrunched her nose up and tried to remember the last time she had a booking.

Last week? Two weeks ago?

She wasn't even sure what day it was. Sometime toward the end of February.

"Oh my darling, oh my darling, oh my darling Clementine. You were lost and gone forever, oh my darling Clementine." She sang to her horse as she scooped poop out of the stall, dumping it into the wheelbarrow that waited in the aisle.

Her phone buzzed again, and she tried to figure out who in the world that could be.

Rick had said good morning to her, but he knew that she would be working, and he wouldn't bother her unless there was a problem.

Was there a problem?

She stopped, leaned the manure fork against the wheelbarrow, and pulled her phone back out of her pants pocket.

There were two texts. Both from her sister, Rita. That was even more strange. Rita knew she didn't have a data plan. She paid for data as she used it with her TracFone. They didn't talk to each other unless it was strictly necessary.

Rick wasn't quite so considerate, and she gave him a little bit of grace, because she figured that when a man liked a woman, he wanted to talk to that girl.

She really wasn't sure how much Rick liked her, and they'd never said anything about being exclusive. Their relationship was one of those ones where she was kind of in limbo all the time, but it suited her just fine, because it wasn't like she was financially stable and ready for a serious boyfriend anyway.

He was. At least he should be. He had a good job, and he was at the point where he could support a wife and family.

She wasn't quite sure he could support a wife with four Clydesdales and a family, but she kinda hoped he was.

A little slice of unease sat on that thought for a moment before she pushed it aside. So life wasn't turning out quite the way she wanted it to. Or the way she thought it was going to. Or the way she had hoped. She had to move on. She couldn't wait around forever for someone who wasn't going to keep his word and who'd ghosted her years ago.

Opening up Rita's text with her nose, she blinked as she read the text, then read it again to be sure.

> I need to talk to you.

The next text was just as mysterious.

> Please. As soon as you can.

That was really weird.

She pulled a glove off with her teeth and held it in her mouth. Should she finish doing the horses? Was this like an emergency where... what? Her sister lived in a suburb of Chicago, and considering their upbringing, she'd done pretty well for herself. She had an apartment and a job, and while she had just broken up with her boyfriend of six months, a six-month relationship wasn't a terrible thing. Considering that Rita hadn't been raised in the best of conditions, it was pretty good that she was as stable as what she was.

She was more stable than Becky anyway.

But Becky had always had more pluck. More grit and determination. There weren't a whole lot of people who could live the way she was living and even enjoy it and be happy about it.

At least that's what she told herself anyway. Still, she decided that this was probably something that she ought to address immediately.

Knowing that she would get cold if she stopped working, she went into the small office, where she allowed herself the luxury of a space heater. She turned it on, pulled her other glove off, and sat on the folding chair in front of the heater so as not to waste any of the glorious warmth coming from it.

She wouldn't have it on for long, just long enough that her fingers wouldn't freeze as she pulled her sister's contact up and put her phone on speaker so she could put her gloves back on and turn the heater off.

"Becky. You didn't have to call me that fast."

"I sure did. You asked me to call you as soon as I could. You know that there isn't too much that I would have been doing that I wouldn't have dropped in order to talk to you right away. What's going on?"

"I got my test results back."

Two

Rita hadn't been feeling the greatest, and Becky had talked her into going to the doctor, who had sent her for a few tests. After all, her job afforded her health insurance, and Becky said she ought to take advantage of it. Whatever it was, it was probably something that would be easily taken care of. At her age, it wouldn't be anything serious, but if a person had insurance that would cover taking care of the little things, she ought to get it done.

She had missed seeing her sister over the holidays, because Rita hadn't felt well, and Becky didn't have anyone dependable with whom she could entrust her horses.

Still, she was looking forward to spring, and she was going to make a point of going to see her sister. It had been way too long, almost a year.

"So what are they saying?" she asked, relieved that Rita had some answers, obviously. Whatever the problem was, they would be able to figure it out; it was the fear of the unknown that usually made things so bad.

"Well, there are a couple of things I didn't tell you."

"Okay," Becky said slowly, reaching over, and against everything that she wanted to do, she turned the heater off.

She sat back, huddled on the chair, holding her phone in her gloved hands. She could see her frozen breath coming out in puffs.

"All right. So the first thing I didn't tell you was that before Brian broke up with me, there was a guy."

"Okay," Becky said, not sure how this had anything to do with anything.

"His name was Chad, and I saw him off and on for about three months."

"He wasn't a drug dealer, was he?" Becky said, knowing that she was using her stern older sister's voice.

"No," Rita said, like it was obvious. "Of course not."

"Okay."

"Well, anyway. I got pregnant."

Becky stilled. Then, she swallowed before she said, "So you had an abortion?" That was the only thing she could think of. After all, Rita hadn't talked about any pregnancy symptoms at all. Although...they didn't talk that much.

"No. And it turned out to be twins."

"Okay," Becky said slowly. They weren't born yet? Was she still pregnant? And why in the world hadn't she told her older sister that she was pregnant, for goodness' sake? After all, wouldn't it have been her job to throw a shower for Rita at the very least? She wanted to celebrate it. Not that she had any money to do any kind of celebrating or even to buy her a pair of booties, but still.

"So, when I told you that I wasn't feeling well, it was on top of the uncomfortableness of pregnancy."

"Okay." Becky couldn't think of anything else to say. She still was missing key pieces of information. She hoped her sister just kept talking.

"Anyway. They did a biopsy. That was the test."

"Okay. A biopsy. Usually I think of that in connotation with cancer. Obviously this is something different."

"No. It's cancer."

Becky sat, stunned. Trying to compute, to figure out what her sister had said, what this meant, and what she was supposed to do.

Suddenly, Becky felt like she wanted to throw up. Forgetting about the cold, she gripped her phone and stood, the folding chair toppling over behind her as she paced from one side of the small office room to the other. There wasn't anything in it other than the chair and the heater, and a small stool on which she kept her record books. Along with a pen. There were no electronic records here. It was her phone, her notebook, and her trusty old pen.

But she wasn't thinking about any of that now.

"You have cancer, or the babies have cancer?"

"I do. They recommended a C-section immediately to take the twins and then have me starting on chemo right away. But...the doctor honestly thought there wasn't much hope. He can save the babies, but he thinks that a C-section might cause the cancer to spread. Sometimes when you operate and you open it up to the air, it...explodes kind of... That wasn't exactly what he said, but it was the picture I got when he was talking."

"So cancer explodes?"

"No...kind of. I don't know. But I scheduled a C-section for this Friday."

"Okay." Becky was running over in her mind what in the world she could do. She had to be there with her sister. She wasn't quite sure how it was going to work out, but she said, "I'll be there."

"Good. Because this is what I need from you."

Wait. Just being there wasn't what she wanted?

"Anything. I'll do anything. Of course I'll do anything for you. You're my sister."

"I love you, Becky. I knew you would say that." Her voice broke, and there was a short pause. "I need you to take my babies."

Wait. She was supposed to take her babies? "Your twins?"

"Yeah. They're almost full term. Thirty-seven weeks. The doctor said they're going to be small, but as far as he can see, they're both healthy, and he doesn't expect any complications for them. For me...he's not sure. The only thing I know for sure is that I'm not going to be able to take care of them right away."

"No, of course not. You gotta fight this cancer."

Rita had cancer. It still hadn't sunk in. Becky was going to have to help her with her twins. That was a little easier to process, even though it was a surprise. But one question stuck in her head. How?

She looked around the small office. Pacing furiously, it was four steps across. Four small steps. This was the only place where she had extra heat. Upstairs...she kept it so cold that even she could barely stand it. Not to mention, it was one room. Her bed, a sink and counter, and a toilet was all together. There was no room for a crib, let alone...two.

"I knew you would help me out." It sounded a little bit like her sister was sniffling or maybe crying. "I don't want to die. But even more, I don't want my babies to die. They didn't ask for this. And I've got to take care of them. You know how things went for us."

"Yeah. I know."

"And I need my babies to have a solid, stable home."

"Of course you do."

"That's why I want Rodney to help you."

Becky paused midstride. "I...thought I told you that I haven't talked to Rodney in years."

"Yes. You had. But Matt knew how to contact him, and I've already spoken with him. He told me yes immediately."

"Wait. You've already talked to Rodney?" She talked to Rodney, Rodney jerk-face Blackstone who ghosted her years ago, after promising her the moon and the stars and all the romantic things, and then totally ditched her? Her sister went to him before she came to Becky?

Becky's fingers had tightened on the phone so much that she was surprised the thing didn't crack.

"Yes. I'm sorry. I knew I could ask and you would do it. You...have so much on your plate. But I want you. I want you more than anyone else. And you and Rodney will take care of my babies like no one else would."

"Of course we will."

She forced the words out, even though her entire heart and soul and spirit and everything within her was rebelling. She was not going to do anything with Rodney. The only way what he did to her would have been acceptable was if he would have been dead. And obviously he wasn't if her sister spoke with him. How dare he. How dare *she*?

She wanted to strangle both of them. And she wasn't normally a violent person.

Well, maybe she was more violent than what she thought, because she didn't want to just strangle Rodney, she wanted to reach into his chest to pull out his beating heart and throw it on the snow and stomp on it and—

Okay. Maybe that was a little much. Even for her.

But that wasn't the important thing. Not right now. Right now, she still hadn't fully grasped that her beloved little sister had...cancer.

"Becky?"

"Yeah?" she said.

"I got the early appointment today so I would know as soon as possible. I...have a bad feeling."

"Of course you do. Cancer would give anyone a bad feeling," Becky said, not wanting to believe for one second that Rita's bad feeling could be anything more than that.

"No. I mean, like a really bad feeling."

"Rita Sue Rivers. You are not going to die. You are going to fight this cancer, and you are going to win. I will take care of your babies, but only on the condition that you are going to fight as hard as you can."

"I'm sorry. You already agreed. You have no room to put any conditions on, because you said you'd do anything for me."

Now Rita sounded like a little sister. Like she was taunting in Becky's face the fact that she had Becky in a hard spot, and knew it, and didn't care.

"Okay. You're right. That's what I said."

"And you've told me a million times that a man is only as good as his word. And you also said, you don't have anything but your word, so it has to be good."

Nothing like having one's words thrown up in one's face when one wanted to go against everything she believed.

She wanted to tell Rita that she would only watch the babies for a set amount of time; that was how long Rita would have to fight the cancer and win.

But she knew those things couldn't have such stipulations put on them, and she also knew that Rita was right. She couldn't put stipulations on anything, because she had promised that she would care for the twins. No matter what. And that she would do anything for Rita.

"I need to go. The doctor's office just emailed me, and I need to look it over. Don't forget, Friday is the C-section."

"I love you," Becky said. Not knowing how she was going to pull any of this off, but her love was stronger than anything else. Her sister was the one thing she had in life that she constantly fought for. And she wasn't going to let her go.

"I love you too."

Becky swiped off on her phone and looked at it for a second, the pain of knowing her sister had a hard road ahead flowing through her. She had to push it aside. She couldn't even think about that, so she focused on the next best thing. Her jaw tightened as she gripped her phone and then threw it as hard as she could into the far corner and screamed at the top of her lungs, "I hate you, Rodney Blackstone!"

It made her feel marginally better.

"That is going to make things rather uncomfortable, I would say."

She spun around, the voice from the doorway of the room startling her. She didn't recognize it immediately.

Not until her gaze landed on the familiar dark eyes, the shock of black hair, the beloved Roman nose, and the strong chin. The face that she had looked to all through her youth for comfort and security and help and for kindness and for everything. He had been her everything. And he had ditched her without looking back.

"Rodney," she said, keeping her hand from going to her throat with the last shred of her self-control. Her eyes narrowed. She hated him. Hated him with a passion.

"Becky." The way he said her name, the way it curled off his tongue, shimmered in the air, slid down her backbone, made something warm want to burst in her chest, but she would not allow it. She squashed it down and narrowed her eyes even further.

"Yeah. Things are going to be uncomfortable." She believed in meeting one's trials head-on, so she marched in high gear toward the doorway, giving Rodney no choice but to step aside. She had horses to take care of.

Three

Rodney stared at Becky's ramrod-straight back. Even with her coat on, he could tell that her muscles were stiff and hard and her back so straight like she had a rod jammed up her spine.

She stomped out to the wheelbarrow and grabbed the handles.

Her movements slowed down as she opened the Clydesdale's stall door, and he thought he heard her ranting under her breath.

When he had thought of all the reunions that he and Becky might have, having it go like this really hadn't been something he considered. He had expected to come back with gifts, a ring possibly, and on his knees, with an apology, a huge, massive, oversized apology, one that she couldn't help but accept, in order to forgive him for what he'd done.

He hoped that what he had done would make sense to her when she heard it, but part of the reason he hadn't contacted her at all in the last five years was because he was afraid that he decided wrong, and he should have told her everything.

In hindsight, it was easy for him to see that would have been the best choice, but at the time, he didn't want anything that would make him look like less in her eyes.

He had two more years until the bankruptcy was off his credit record, and it could be buried forever. Or at least as buried as it would ever get. He thought he would wait two more years before he came to see her. Two more years to multiply the millions he'd made in the last five into perhaps a billion.

Becky, being the stubborn, willful, faithful girl that she was, wouldn't ever be with anyone else. He was sure of that. She had told him she was devoted to him, and even if he disappeared from the face of the earth, she would never go back on her word.

But now, he had no ring, no big apology, no over-the-top gift, and it was freezing in here.

He had been spending most of his time in LA, and the climate shock was...massive, to say the least.

"Have you spoken with your sister?" he asked as he walked over. He knew that was the one thing she would talk to him about. If Rita had talked to her about taking care of the twins while Rita dealt with whatever it was she needed to deal with. She hadn't told him. All she said was that she was going to be delivering twins on Friday and that she was not going to be able to take care of them right away. And she wanted them to be cared for by Becky and him.

Of course, he would give Rita anything she wanted, because he knew Becky doted on her. He hadn't even asked how she had found his number or what had made her think that this was a good idea. Because he knew nothing about children and even less about babies, other than it was always nice when someone else was doing something with them, and he was not.

"That's who was on the phone."

"That's who was on the phone that caused you to throw it against the wall and scream that you hated me?" That made sense. She had just been asked to take care of babies alongside him. Well, if he'd wondered how she felt about him, now he knew. And if he'd wondered how she was going to feel about taking care of her sister's children with him, he had a pretty clear picture of that as well.

He'd made some dumb mistakes in his life, a couple that made him lose the fortune that he had spent ten years amassing, but typically he wasn't stupid.

"Yeah. That was the cause of that little outburst." She looked up at him, gave him an absolutely fake, saccharine smile, and then went back into the horse's stall. She knew as well as he did that it was dangerous to work around horses when one was angry or upset. They were very sensitive to people's feelings, and quick movements were liable to make an already jumpy horse do something that could put a person's life in danger. Not that a horse, especially a Clydesdale who were known for their gentle, calm demeanor, would hurt someone on purpose, but a horse often wasn't thinking about hurting anyone when they were just trying to get away from what they perceived as danger.

"I came as soon as she called me. Which was last night, late. She said she was getting test results back this morning, and she wasn't sure what they were going to be, but she knew that she was going to need us."

"Great. That was basically what she told me too," Becky said, not looking up at him and not stopping her work.

She took the forkful of manure, dumped it in the wheelbarrow, and went back for another one.

"Can't you stop working and look at me?" he asked, frustrated.

"Sure. Soon as I'm done here, because I've got a lot of things to do today, and I don't have time to mess around with you."

"I would have thought that not having spoken with me for five years, you'd be a little curious."

"No. You not having spoken with me for the last five years made me not want to talk to you ever again." She said it like it was the most natural thing in the world.

He had obviously underestimated the strength of her feelings.

Who was it that said there was a fine line between love and hate?

It seemed like Becky's love for him had turned into hate. And since she didn't know all the details, she had a right to feel that way. Even if she did know the details, she had a right to feel however she wanted to. Of course, a person of character did not act on the way they felt but on what they knew to be right.

"Becky, we're going to have to get along, just because we're going to have Rita's babies together. Unless you told her you wouldn't do it because it was with me?"

"No. She conned me into telling her that I would do anything for her, all she had to do was ask. I said that before I realized she was going to ask me to do something with you. Otherwise, the answer would have been a resounding no and probably a heck no."

The Becky he knew growing up might have put some profanity in there. But as they went through their teenage years, Becky had seemed to develop a closer and closer relationship with the Lord, while Rodney had drifted away. That was partly due to his parents. His father had cheated. He flinched when he thought about the murder-suicide and losing both of his parents. Even though they had not been great parents, he had struggled for a while. Of course. But Becky had always been there to anchor him, to ground him, to remind him of what was right and good and beautiful in the world.

He had some help from the folks in Strawberry Sands as well, and Matt had helped him get into horses. That, along with Becky, and her pointing him constantly to the Lord, had pulled him out of what had been almost sure to be a downward spiral that ended in tragedy.

Then, because he dealt with Cord Stryker in Sweet Water, North Dakota, a billionaire who lived there, Ford Hansen, had taken him under his wing and taught him about business.

But he'd grown too big too fast, because he'd been in a hurry to get rich and get back to Becky, and he'd lost it all five years ago, declaring bankruptcy.

Ford Hansen could have saved him, but as Ford explained later, he wouldn't have learned the lessons he needed to rebuild faster and better than he had before.

He appreciated what Ford had done, truly did, but...he'd been so ashamed that he hadn't been successful the first time out of the gate that he had stopped talking to Becky, who had continued to keep up a correspondence with him throughout all the time he'd been under Ford's tutelage.

It was his fault that he was standing here now with her spitting-nails mad and him having absolutely no idea of how to handle it. Becky had never been furious at him. She'd been angry plenty of times but never to the point he couldn't talk to her.

Becky was still storming in and out of the stall, cleaning with an intensity that he doubted she'd shown in years. He dared any poop to try to elude her.

Silently of course.

"All right. I can see you're busy. When will you have time to talk?"

"I don't see that we have anything to talk about," she said. And to his surprise, he was pretty sure she meant it.

"We're supposedly raising your sister's twins together. At least until she gets whatever it is figured out that she needs to figure it out."

"She has cancer, Rodney." Becky stopped long enough to spit those words at him, then narrowed her gaze as he felt his mouth open and his eyes widen.

Becky was losing her sister. No wonder she was acting the way she was. She probably didn't know how to handle her grief and sadness and fear. So it was all coming out as anger.

He could understand that. He struggled for a long time with anger of his own. Becky had been instrumental in helping him. She pointed him to Jesus, which was what he needed. She never made it about herself. She had always been humble. It was one of the things that he loved about her. Feisty, gritty, determined—i.e., stubborn—but never proud. Ever.

He walked toward her, choosing to stand in front of her so she had no choice but to stop as he put one hand on the wall and one hand on his hip.

"Get outta my way," she said. Not meeting his eyes.

"I'm sorry to hear that your sister has cancer. She either didn't know or didn't tell me last night on purpose. She let me think it was just going to be for a little while."

Becky sighed, a put-out sound that let him know that she was listening but not willingly. And he needed to hurry up.

"Regardless, that makes it even more imperative that you and I talk. When will it work for you?"

"Maybe Wednesday. Sometime in the afternoon."

Her words were clipped, her body turned slightly away from him, and her tone saying that she didn't care what he wanted.

"Wednesday?" he repeated, unable to believe that she didn't have a single moment until then.

"I can meet you at the diner in Blueberry Beach. I have to go down for groceries and pick up some feed anyway."

"All right. I'll drive."

"No. I can meet you there." She met his gaze headlong, in a challenge.

Should he let it go? He couldn't exactly force her to ride with him, but...

He probably should pick his battles. He too had made a promise to Rita before she had let him know that she wanted him to do something with Becky. Something along the lines of, "You're like a sister to me. I'll do whatever you ask."

Well, what was the saying about repenting at leisure? It looked like he was going to have a good long while to wish that he had been a little bit more inquisitive about what exactly she was going to want him to do.

Becky was obviously not in the mood to deal with him. But maybe the fact that they were going to have to do something with these babies together would help heal the hurt he'd inflicted on her. She was loyal to a fault. More loyal than anyone he'd ever met. But obviously he had broken her trust, and there was a flipside to that loyalty: her ability to hold a grudge longer and deeper than anyone he ever knew.

Of course, as a Christian, she knew that wasn't right, and she'd tried to moderate that side of her personality back when she was younger. He wouldn't be surprised if by Wednesday, her anger had dissipated and she was a lot more reasonable. Probably it was a good idea to wait to talk until then.

"All right. I'll meet you at the diner in Blueberry Beach. Twelve okay?"

"Two." Now he thought she was just being contrary.

But he knew how to handle contrary people. After all, Ford had taught him the art of negotiating since that had an awful lot to do with a person's ability to make money.

"All right. Two. At the Blueberry Beach diner. I'll be there."

"Yeah, I've heard that before."

He had started to turn away. He knew her jab was designed to hurt him. It succeeded. She was right. She had heard him make promises before, heard him say that he would be somewhere for her. And he'd broken those promises. He thought he had good reason, but... Becky probably wouldn't agree.

"You can count on it, sweetheart."

"I am not your sweetheart," she said, throwing the manure she had on her fork into the wheelbarrow so forcefully some of it spilled out the other side.

He looked at it, then looked up at her, but she had already spun on her heel and stomped away.

He'd thought for a while that his life was full and busy, and he wanted it that way, because he only gave himself two more years to make whatever money he was going to make so that he could come back to Becky, wealthy and successful, and ask her to marry him, finally.

He had a feeling he hadn't known what busy was.

Four

Becky was so steamed she could hardly stand it. The idea, the nerve, the absolute gall of Rodney to show up at the barn and think that she wouldn't have anything to say about the fact that he'd been radio silent for five whole years.

Despite the pleading texts she sent to him. The letters that had been returned unopened, the phone calls she made that had gone to some kind of recording saying that the number had been disconnected.

And now, and *now* he decides to come and talk to her?

Ha. Like she would ever.

Except she had to.

The one nice thing about horses, well, one of the many nice things about horses in her opinion, was they forced a person to calm down. To be deliberate in their movements, to not allow their emotions to affect their actions.

Becky remembered this as Velvet, the least calm of all of her horses, trotted around the round pen.

She was lunging her, as she did almost on a daily basis, to keep her horses in shape and to get a little exercise. She wished she could put them out in the pasture, but currently there was a crust on the ice. Her horses would most likely break through because of their weight, but she didn't want to chance the fact that if they didn't, they could slide and break something.

She personally had made sure that the round pen had been cleared of ice as well as snow. Her horses were too valuable to her for her to chance allowing them to get hurt. Of course, it made extra work for her, but it was worth it.

She had as many house-cleaning jobs as she could, and she picked up any extra jobs that were available anywhere near Raspberry Ridge.

Her pickup was not very reliable, and she couldn't afford to fix it if it broke down, so the only time she ran it was when she had to go to Blueberry Beach to pick up feed. She added groceries to that, because she thought it made more sense for her to make one trip, rather than one for the horses and an additional one for food for herself. But the beans and rice she bought last month were holding out nicely. Even if they were getting rather old with nothing else to go with them.

Although she got coffee, too. She did splurge for that. She felt like she needed it though, in these cold temperatures. She had to do something to help keep herself warm. She'd lost twenty pounds over the winter, and she hadn't had that much extra to begin with.

Still, she had to calm herself down in order to work with horses properly and not upset them. So she tried to think rationally about the situation.

She didn't want to process the fact that her sister had cancer. Apparently a not-good form of it, if they were worried about it "exploding." Which she had never heard of, but her sister had said that those weren't the words that the doctor had used exactly, it was just her takeaway from it.

That made her want to drop everything and race to her sister's side. But she was still faced with the fact that she didn't have anyone to take care of her horses. She had a couple of people she thought she could ask, but it was going to be a big inconvenience for them, especially with the hard winter they had faced so far. Every week, there had been a snowstorm, and sometimes two. They'd gotten more than six feet of snow, which was a record in some places, including Raspberry Ridge.

Still, she was not afraid to ask for favors, because it was her sister.

But it occurred to her, when Velvet was done and back in her stall and Jethro was on the line, that…Rodney was going to find out just how desperate her circumstances were. There really was no way he couldn't. Because if they did what she wanted, which was she would keep the babies for a week, and then he would keep the babies for a week, or something along those lines, he was going to have to figure out that…she couldn't afford to feed herself, let alone two babies.

While her sister had work, it wasn't a great job. She wasn't going to be able to shower her with money to buy things for the babies. She was going to need formula at the very least, and after she stopped, stuck the lunge line under her arm, and googled baby formula, she understood that there was no way she was going to be able to afford to feed those babies. Just no way.

Actually, there was a way, but she didn't want to think about that right now.

But for her sister, she would.

Still, Rodney was going to find out. He was going to see how desperate she was. How poor, and while it didn't really bother her, not terribly anyway, because she was doing what she always wanted to do and loved, it did bother her that he would think she wasn't successful. That she hadn't done anything worthwhile with her life. That… whatever bad thing it was he was going to think. He would look at her and think she was a failure. And be glad that he didn't have anything to do with her.

Maybe that was what turned him against her in the first place. He saw that she was unmotivated and didn't care about making money, which seemed to be his focus, more and more and more, and maybe the more he focused on it, the less she did.

Maybe she was naturally the balance to him. Without even thinking about it.

She shook her head. She did not want to think that was true in any way. She didn't want to balance Rodney in anything. She didn't want to do anything with him.

"Good boy, Jethro." Jethro was the laziest of her horses. He did not move any faster than a slow walk unless she pressed him the whole time.

He was more than happy to stop and did so in his tracks. Not going one step farther than what he had to.

She walked over, rubbing under his mane at the special spot that he just loved to have scratched. Then, she wound up the lunge line, snapping the lead rope on, taking the lunge line off, before she led him back to his stall.

He towered over her, making her feel tiny, but he was so gentle, so sweet, so loving that she was not afraid, ever. Even when he was upset. Which wasn't very often.

She couldn't imagine life without her beloved horses.

She finished, checking down over her outfit to make sure that she wasn't too dirty and changing out of her barn boots into her worn pair of cowboy boots.

They weren't nearly as warm, and they were terrible in the snow, but she was heading out to clean Vera and Dominic's house, and she didn't want to show up with horse poop all over her shoes.

She didn't bother to go upstairs to get anything to eat, even though her stomach growled. Sometimes Vera would tell her to help herself to some snacks or leftovers that she had on the counter. Becky always tried not to eat too much, but she preferred to have her one meal of the day at the end of the day so she could go to bed with a warm, full belly. That helped to make it so that she didn't feel the cold in her room quite as much.

She brushed off the couple of inches of snow that they'd gotten last night from the windshield of her truck, and then she climbed in. She always left the keys in it. There wasn't anyone around who would steal it, but even if there were, if they were desperate enough to steal a truck that looked like hers, she kind of felt like maybe they needed it more than she did.

"Come on, Rod, start for me."

Like an idiot, when she'd gotten the truck, she'd named it after Rodney. Rodney never went by Rod, but that's what she called her truck.

She probably should change the name, but she identified with it now and didn't really think of Rodney all that much when she said it.

Which was a lie. She thought of him all the time. But it was also a fact that it would be like changing a child's name after they'd had it for ten years. They just wouldn't seem like the same person.

Anyway, she turned the key, and the motor chugged slowly.

She pumped the gas a few times, said another prayer, and then whispered a bit of encouragement before she tried again.

It sounded a little better that time but still wasn't catching.

"One more time. You gotta get me to town. I'm supposed to get paid today. I need money to buy feed on Wednesday. Come on."

Maybe Rod heard her, or maybe it was the Lord, but the truck started to life.

"Thank you, Jesus." She wasn't confused about why the truck started. And it had nothing to do with the fact that she had it named, and she talked to it. But everything to do with the fact that sometimes God still smiled on her.

A lot of times actually. She was really happy with her life for the most part. Well, had been happy about it until her sister's phone call this morning. And now, it felt like her entire life had descended into chaos. Her sister had cancer. And was pregnant with twins. And to make everything a million times worse, Rodney. Here.

She wanted to cry. She wasn't really that angry at him. She was more hurt than anything. She could admit that to herself, although she'd never admit it to him. Or anybody else. How could he do that to her? Why couldn't he just say, "Hey, I'm a little more sophisticated than you are now, and you're too childish for me"?

Even though she was almost thirty. Still, he was a good bit older than her, and he always seemed so much more mature.

Nothing had changed in that regard, considering how much of an idiot she had acted like today when she had been so angry she couldn't even talk to him.

Why hadn't she just talked to him in the barn, rather than deciding to meet on Wednesday, at the diner in Blueberry Beach, no less? What was she, a glutton for punishment? It would have been far better to hash it out today, in fifteen or twenty minutes, than have to spend an entire meal eating across from him.

She gasped. She hadn't even considered that she was going to have to pay for that meal.

She was not going to let Rodney buy it.

But she really couldn't afford to eat in a restaurant. It was all she could do to afford the beans and rice she had at home.

She pressed her lips together. She didn't even have his number to be able to call him to cancel.

What had she been thinking?

She put the truck in reverse after giving it a minute to warm up and laughed at herself.

She hadn't been thinking anything. First, her sister dropped her news of her pregnancy and then her cancer, and then Rodney. Obviously, she'd been overwhelmed. But she was an adult. She was supposed to be able to handle being overwhelmed. She wasn't supposed to melt down over a day like she had. Although, she doubted she'd ever have a day like that again.

Then she laughed. With twins—she was going to be raising twins, for a while anyway—probably today was actually a calm, easy day compared to that.

Although Rodney would be helping her. That calmed her soul a bit, until she remembered that she was going to specifically request that Rodney not co-parent with her. They would switch the kids back and forth the way divorced people did. Because she couldn't stand to do it any other way.

She pulled into Vera's and shut the motor off. It was so nice to feel the heat from the heater that she almost let it run a little bit.

But it would be warm in Vera's house, and she would be able to shed some of her layers.

Typically, Vera took the kids down to the basement and played with them down there while Becky cleaned; that way, everyone was out from underfoot. Otherwise, Vera said, Becky cleaned, and her kids just came behind her and messed everything back up.

Becky really didn't mind. It made things more interesting when the kids were underfoot, but it did make it harder as well. Because they all wanted to help too. Which was fun, but she was getting paid to clean, not follow behind a two-year-old with a mop pretending to clean.

She wasn't sure how many kids Vera and Dominic had. It changed, since they fostered some, who went in and out. Right now, they had a toddler and a preschooler, along with their older children.

She'd never met such bighearted people, and Vera was one of her heroes.

Taking a deep breath, she yanked on the door latch and shoved her shoulder against it to get the door open. It complied with a shriek, and it almost felt like it was complaining about the cold, which Becky could not fault it for.

After this, she had the church to clean, which was always a fun and peaceful time. And then she had to check in on Mr. Harris, who lived by himself. He only had a woodstove for heat, and Becky made sure that he had chopped wood brought into the house every day. He didn't really pay her a whole lot. But she couldn't quit that job. Mr. Harris's children wanted to send him to a home, and he was trying as hard as he could to stay in the home he loved. He was in a sound mind and in pretty good physical condition, but at his age, which was eighty-eight, it was not a good idea for him to go outside and get his own firewood. Especially in the winter after it had snowed.

So, she shoveled the walk, made sure that his paper had been brought in, and that he had firewood. Occasionally she grabbed groceries for him too. She would get the groceries more if she could afford to spend the money on it.

Seeing the day's work stretch out ahead of her, she trudged up the walk to get started.

Five

"I don't really like to say I told you so, but... I told you so." Davis stood looking at Rodney. Davis and Matt Landry had been instrumental in Rodney's upbringing, after his dad had cheated on his mother and his parents had died.

Matt had helped him with the horses he got interested in, mostly because of Becky, but he'd loved them himself. Which had led him to Cord Stryker, which had led him to Ford Hansen in Sweet Water, North Dakota. It was funny how life just worked out, and he could see God's hand through it all.

"I really thought she'd understand," he finally said. Davis had told him to just admit to Becky what happened. That he'd overextended himself, taken a gamble, because that's what being in business was, and he failed. Big time. Lost everything. And had to declare bankruptcy.

He had started to rebuild before the ashes had settled, but that moved the timeline that he had set for him coming back and asking Becky to marry him.

He'd been so depressed, so desperate, so embarrassed that he quit talking to her altogether.

Matt had a long conversation with him, after Becky came to him crying because Rodney wasn't communicating with her.

Rodney had held fast. He didn't want Becky to see him like this. He had been telling her how successful he was, bragging some, just wanting her to know that she was getting a guy who was successful and that she could be proud of.

"She would have understood if you told her right away. Women don't like it when their guy hides things from them. But it is what it is now," Matt said, making a smacking sound with his lips as he thoughtfully turned away from Rodney and looked out the window.

Another snowstorm was coming down hard, and it was going to make travel to the Chicago suburbs treacherous. But he had business he needed to take care of before he came back up to meet with Becky Wednesday afternoon.

"How is Becky doing?" Davis asked. "She became a little distant since she lost contact with you. She checks in once in a while, but I don't hear from her regularly like we used to."

It was surprising to Rodney. He hadn't realized that. She wasn't that far away up in Raspberry Ridge, but he supposed winter with this kind of snow made any distance a distance that no one wanted to travel.

"She looked fine. She was angry, but...fine. She has four beautiful Clydesdales, and she was taking good care of them."

The Clydesdales looked like they were in excellent health, which told Rodney that she had enough money to feed her horses, so she was probably eating okay too.

It was hard to tell what she looked like underneath her bulky winter clothes, but obviously she was up and working, and angry. Very angry.

"I knew she had horses," Davis said thoughtfully. "She got them a few years ago. They are her pride and joy. The culmination of years of dreams."

"What does she do with them? Give carriage rides on the beach?" Rodney asked. He was desperate for any information on Becky, but he hadn't really wanted to admit that he didn't know anything. As in, no contact for years.

"Yeah. She was trying to build a business of giving carriage rides. Not just horseback riding along the beach. She had to choose one or the other, because she couldn't afford to keep her riding horses and get the Clydesdales."

Davis said this casually, although Rodney felt like he could read between the lines. He bet that Davis either had given Becky a loan for the horses, or knew who had.

And if he knew Becky, she'd pay back every cent, with interest. Even if she had to take it out of her blood.

He looked around the well-appointed study. The deep mahogany bookshelves were filled, almost overflowing, with books on a variety of different subject matters. Davis was an excellent businessman, and he was widely read. He was one of the smartest people that Rodney knew. Very savvy. Ford Hansen had him beat hands down. Still, they were equally kind, equally bighearted, and they had equally wonderful wives.

Both of them would tell him in an instant that his choice of wife would make or break his life. After all, it was the single most important decision a man would make after choosing to follow the Lord.

Matt, who, with his wife Jubilee, owned a riding stable along the lake and rented out riding horses throughout the summer for tourists, was also a savvy businessman. But his interests were more geared toward his family, and he wasn't as wealthy as Davis. But in wisdom, he was just as rich.

These were two of Rodney's favorite people in the world and the men who had come along beside him, even giving him a place to stay, when he had gone through his difficult teenage years. He almost veered off the straight and narrow, but along with Becky, these guys had kept him honest.

"I guess I don't know what to do. She was so angry at me she wouldn't talk. She did agree to meet with me at the diner in Blueberry Beach on Wednesday, but...she didn't seem like she was going to be very forgiving."

"Well, I don't know that I have a whole lot of good advice for you. Just be honest and humble. And apologetic."

"I guess I have to agree. I definitely feel like it's best to be honest from the beginning. It's harder to get yourself out of a hole once you've dug it around yourself and fallen into it."

Rodney had to wonder what in the world he was thinking about at the time, because in hindsight, he could see that Davis and Matt were absolutely right. But at the time, he had been dead set against Becky ever finding out about what had happened. Now, it was time to face the piper, and with so much happening, he wasn't sure that he was going to be able to give Becky the attention she deserved. After all, he was still trying to run a business, and he was going to somehow have twins to take care of.

Hopefully Becky would do the heavy lifting on that, and he would pay for things. Although... He had no idea how she was expecting to break it down. If she was trying to run a business, she probably wasn't going to have any more time to take care of two babies than he did. Perhaps they would both have to make sacrifices. Somehow, he thought he was probably more equipped to do that than she was.

"Beyond Becky, I've never wanted to let anyone who's invested in me down. You two, and Ford Hansen, are among the top. Cord helped me get started with the horses, but Becky took that all over."

"When you stopped talking to her, she got completely away from your horses."

That was true. He'd ended up having to sell them. He hadn't wanted to, but it had actually been helpful, because it had given him some of the money he needed in order to pay his previous creditors off. He had to declare bankruptcy, but he had paid back every cent he owed.

"I remember you being concerned when you got out of the horses, that Cord Stryker would be upset with you. He wasn't," Matt said, lifting a brow, as though daring Rodney to remember.

"You're right," he said easily, grimacing a bit when he remembered how nervous he had been to go see him. He'd been so afraid that he was going to be upset after all of the time and effort that Cord had put into him. Instead, he'd been happy, wishing him well, telling him if he ever needed anything to not be afraid to knock on his door, because he'd help with anything he could.

"I think the generosity and kindness of people sometimes surprise us. Sure, people get mad about stuff and that surprises us too, but you have some really good people around you. Ford is not going to be disappointed in you if you don't make one billion. He would be more disappointed in you if you didn't take care of Becky's sister's twins." Davis raised his brows. "And I know I'm proud of what you've done. I'm proud of the way you handled yourself when things didn't go well for you. I'm proud of how you made sure that you paid everyone back. Because it would have been easier to walk away. I'm proud of how you got up from the ashes, prayed about it, and then dove right back in. There aren't a lot of people with grit like that."

"He's friends with Becky. He really doesn't have any choice but to have grit like that."

The men laughed, but Rodney also cringed a bit inside. Right now, Becky would not consider him her friend.

He could almost hear her saying, friends stayed in touch. Friends didn't ghost their friends. Friends talked to their friends when they had a problem. Friends gave their friends their phone numbers. Friends didn't walk away from their friends.

"In all seriousness, you can't worry about letting people down." Matt nodded at Rodney, as though trying to get him to agree.

He knew that Davis and Matt were right. Ford wasn't going to be upset, and obviously they weren't either. He had millions made already, and he had his fingers in a bunch of different pots to continue making money. But it was almost like when someone was starting out, they had to put their heart and soul and everything they had into building. A person couldn't build a multimillion-dollar empire by fiddling around with other things. They had to go deep with everything they had.

But he was already more than successful. He'd already made more fortunes than most men saw in a lifetime. He could stop. He could stop where he was, and yeah, he wouldn't have reached any of his goals, but no one who saw him would think that he wasn't successful. Except, his mentors had known that his dream was to be a billionaire, not just a millionaire, and he was going to stop short of that, hence his fear of letting people down.

But Davis and Matt were right. No one who knew him was going to be upset. They were all going to say that he was choosing the better thing. It was one thing to put your heart and soul into something when you didn't have people who depended on you. But now was the time for him to step up, maybe like he should have done five years ago, and be there for Becky. And her sister, and her twins.

"Are the twins girls or boys or one of each?" Matt asked, completely changing the subject.

"You know, I never even thought to ask. I was just so flabbergasted that she had cancer and that she was pregnant. I didn't know."

"I didn't know either." Matt lifted a shoulder. "She might have been trying to keep it quiet, because she was ashamed."

Rodney nodded. Considering that she and Becky had always said they wanted better for their kids, it was more than possible, but he didn't say anything more.

They talked about a few other things, but Rodney really did need to get to Chicago. Especially if he was going to wind things down. After talking to these men, he really thought he should. He needed to step out of his mindset of building wealth and think instead about building family. He was pretty sure that Becky would come around, and the two of them would figure things out. After all, he waited his whole life for her. She was the only one he wanted. And as far as he knew, she'd done the same for him. Of course, they hadn't talked in the last five years, but he couldn't imagine that anything had truly changed.

Six

Tuesday night, after finishing up the horse chores, Becky took the small space heater upstairs and used some of the precious heat to warm the area where her shower was.

It wasn't really a shower. It was an old-fashioned metal washtub with a shower curtain on a wire around the top of it and an old spigot that doubled as a showerhead with hot and cold water that splashed down in it.

She would have to empty the tub when she was done, but it served to get her clean, although this winter, she was embarrassed to admit how seldom she used it. Not only was it freezing cold in her small apartment, but taking all the layers of clothes off and then having all the work to empty the tub made it so that for her to take a shower, she really, really had to want one.

But she and Rick were going to the snowmobile races tonight, and for some reason, it was extremely important that Rick look at her with... maybe not love, but admiration or something. Not disgust. She didn't want him to wrinkle up his nose and ask her how long it had been since she'd been in her old metal washtub. Which was how he politely asked how long it had been since she showered.

Snowmobile races were not her favorite, but Rick liked them, so she went with him. Plus, it was something to do on the long winter evenings, and it got her out of her apartment. Even though her heart longed to be with her sister, Rita had insisted she was fine and would rather Becky use her favors to have people take care of her horses when the twins were born. Going out would take her mind off Rita and the cancer and the kids she didn't know how she was going to afford to care for.

Not that she minded being by herself. She really didn't. And if she got lonely, her horses weren't far away.

But the more she thought about it, the more she thought that the one thing she could do to help her sister out was to sell her horses, and it was selfish of her not to.

But selling her horses not only meant losing the best friends she had but also giving up her dreams of having her own business. It was...hard to think about. Because it was all she had wanted since before she had graduated from high school. Still, there was no way she could take care of twin babies right now. So, while she was going to wait to talk to Rodney and see what he said, she was almost certain that that was what she was going to have to do.

Really, she would rather spend the night with her horses than at the snowmobile races, but she bundled up and was waiting at the barn door when Rick pulled up in his jacked-up, tricked-out truck.

He was so proud of it, and he spent all of his extra money on it.

It was part of the reason she figured their relationship hadn't gotten any more serious than what it had. He didn't have enough money for a girlfriend and the truck. So, he had Becky, who was an almost girlfriend and was content there, since she didn't have money for a boyfriend and her horses.

They were very similar in that regard. She was pretty sure that was where their similarities ended, but Rick was nice to her, and he wasn't a mean drunk, which was saying something, because finding a guy who didn't consume copious amounts of alcohol any time he wasn't working was rather hard to do.

Becky had never seen alcohol make anyone act smarter, and she'd seen it make a lot of people do a lot of dumb things. Which was enough to convince her that she didn't want to have anything to do with it.

But to each his own, she supposed, though there were a ton of biblical principles that she could apply to the idea that one should not indulge.

Regardless, he wouldn't drink and drive, so he wouldn't be drinking right now. Although, more than once she'd ended up driving his truck home while he crashed in her driveway until he was sober enough to drive home in the morning.

Hopefully tonight would not be one of those nights.

He pulled up to the barn and laid on the horn.

She hurried out and got in the truck. He preferred not to have to get out. Not only because he would be wearing cowboy boots and it would be slippery for him to walk around in them, but also because it was cold out, and he didn't like the cold.

She wasn't sure why he lived in Michigan. He should have migrated to a warmer climate long ago, as much as he complained about the cold.

"Man. It's colder than a preacher's wife on Saturday night," he said as she got in.

"It is chilly," she said. Rick was not Rodney. She and Rodney had intellectual discussions that were stimulating and fun, they got each other's humor, and they gently teased each other while never being derogatory toward each other. She had loved their interactions and the friendship they shared.

She would not necessarily call Rick a friend, although she knew if she needed him, she could call him. He might not come, but he was definitely someone she could call.

She didn't particularly enjoy talking to him, and they didn't share any of the same interests. He didn't care for her Clydesdales at all. If he liked any horses, they were quarter horses and had to do with the rodeo, although he wasn't really a rodeo guy. He was a truck dude. And he was good at what he did. He was a mechanic, and he worked on other people's trucks as well as his own. He wasn't afraid to work, she would give him that. But he also played hard.

Even as she said it, she knew she was just kidding herself. Rick wasn't her friend. He wasn't even an almost boyfriend. He was just the best she thought she could do. After Rodney ditched her, she realized that she really never had another friend like him. She was too...caustic? Determined? Tough?

Something like that. She intimidated men and wasn't all that lovable. So, when Rick showed a little bit of interest, she jumped at the opportunity. Certainly it was the best she was going to get.

There. That was the honest truth.

"I can't wait to go. Last week, it was canceled because of the snow, and the rematch between the Green Machine and Buzzyear Blue Boy has been a long time coming. Lavoie just got his machine back up and running last week."

"Oh," she said, not really caring but not knowing how to answer him.

He rambled on, and on and on, and she didn't really have to worry about saying much till they got to the track.

The bleachers were out in the open, and she supposed that's why the alcohol sales were so good. It was hard to sit there in the cold and dark stone-cold sober.

"You got a problem with driving home, darlin'?" Rick asked as he pulled out a can of snuff and settled a pinch in his cheek.

"No. I can do that," she said.

She yanked her door handle and remembered just in time that the drop was much bigger than just a little step. She grabbed a hold of the handle and slid to the ground.

"Hey, babe, I'm a little low this week. Would you pay to get us in? If you don't, I'm not going to have enough for the alcohol I'm going to need in order to stay warm tonight." He grinned at her. "Unless you want to keep me warm." His voice dropped a little, and she was shaking her head no before he even stopped talking. Mostly to disguise the disgusting shiver that went through her.

"No, that's okay. Okay."

She had her wallet tucked inside her coat pocket, but she'd done that more out of habit than thinking that she was going to need to use it tonight.

Her credit card was maxed out, but she had enough in her checking account to cover the feed she had been planning on buying the next day.

She did some quick calculations in her head, and if she didn't eat anything at all tonight and didn't spend any money at the diner when she met with Rodney on Wednesday, she would just be a dollar short.

It would cost her thirty-five dollars if she overdrew her account, and she hated to do that for just a dollar, but...she wasn't sure what else to do.

"Do you have a dollar in quarters in your ashtray?" she asked as they walked toward the ticket booth.

"Probably. I just threw some change in there. Although, I don't usually pay with cash too much anymore."

"Do you mind if I grab four quarters out later?"

He didn't even ask why. He just put an arm around her and jiggled her, kind of roughly. "Sure, babe. Anything for you."

He said that, but she knew it as sure as she was standing there that he didn't mean it.

She would feel ridiculous going to the bank and putting four quarters in her account, but...that was better than the thirty-five-dollar overdraft fee.

Satisfied that she could do it, she got her debit card out and paid for their tickets, and then waited while Rick bought himself a supersized beer, plus the extra-large nachos with cheese, and a bowl of chili.

"Hey, babe. I can't carry all this. Can you get the nachos?" He grinned at her. "I'll not ask you to hold my beer." He laughed, like it was funny. She thought there might be some kind of social cues in there that were supposed to be humorous, but it went over her head.

"Sure," she said, coming over and taking the nachos from him.

"Oh shoot, babe. I didn't get you anything. You want something?"

He had a beer in one hand and his chili in the other, and even though he asked her, he kept walking toward the stands fast enough that she had to take a couple of jogging steps to catch up.

She never answered him, and he never asked again.

"Hey, there's the gang. We want to get that front-row seat right there. There's two left. Actually, there might not be quite enough room for you. You can sit behind me, babe. That'll keep me warmer anyway." He grinned down at her and then leaned forward and slid into the front-row seat, assuming she'd take the seat behind him without looking. Once he was seated, he reached back for his nachos.

"Want to eat these before they freeze," he said, snickering like it was funny.

She was pretty cold by the time the race was over. Rick had had five supersized beers and made four trips to the restroom.

She was pretty sure he stood by the tire and peed again before he got in the truck, but she got in and started it, being careful not to look, loving the feel of driving a vehicle that started the first time she turned the key and luxuriating in that.

Regardless, she was going to be long gone by the time morning came around and would not know whether there was yellow snow beside the tire or not. One of the great mysteries of life that she was content to not solve.

Rick was not a loud drunk, but it had been a big evening, and after he climbed in the cab—on his third try—he promptly fell asleep, snoring loudly.

She would get out at her place, and he wouldn't even wake up. She'd let the truck run so he wouldn't freeze to death overnight. It was old enough that it didn't have one of those automatic shutoffs after twenty minutes. Whoever designed those didn't have a drunk boyfriend apparently.

Actually, she knew what the rest of the world did with their boyfriends, but...that wasn't her.

At least it never had been. But she supposed she'd been skating closer and closer to that line for a while now.

It wouldn't surprise her if sometime Rick tried to come in after one of their "dates" just because he thought it was his right.

Thankfully, by the time the dates were over, he was usually too drunk to try to kiss her, which suited her just fine. But as she was driving home in the dark, with the white Michigan landscape stretching out as far as the headlights shone, she thought that if she was going to be raising her sister's twins, especially if something happened to her little sister and it became a permanent thing, she didn't really want them in this kind of environment. She didn't want them with a guy who got drunk every time he went out, who was addicted to nicotine, and who had the manners of an alley cat with the spitting and the peeing and the disregard for the barest of gentlemanly conduct.

How was she going to raise children to be different if that's who she hung around?

But she was going to be doing it with Rodney, and having Rick between them would be a buffer. It would let him know that she wasn't completely disposable, like he had acted. The way he ditched her without a word. That someone actually did want her. Even if it was someone like Rick.

So, she had her vanity, where she wanted to keep Rick around, just so that Rodney would know she was worth something, but what would be best for the twins would be to ditch Rick as quick and fast as she could, never see him or his cronies again. Not if she wanted to raise those twins right.

So, she had a decision to make, the same as selling her horses.

And she knew, as much as she didn't want to, she knew what she was going to decide. She had to. She just couldn't do anything else. It would practically kill her to list her horses for sale, but it was what she had to do in order to do the best for the twins and her sister. So, when she parked the truck, she got the four quarters out of the ashtray, and then upon further reflection, she took one more. Maybe it was stealing, or maybe it was payment for the ride home. That's how she wanted to think about it. She didn't like to think that she'd stolen anything, even $0.25. But she pulled out the pen that she always kept in her wallet, and then she grabbed a check out of her checkbook. She wrote "void" on the front and then wrote a small note on the back.

I took $1.25.
I can pay you
back if you
want me to.

She chewed on the end of the pen. Rick snorted, shifted, and then went back to snoring.

She held her breath until the snores were even again. She really didn't want to talk to him. She didn't feel like she was exactly breaking up. As far as she knew, the entire time they'd dated, Rick hadn't dated anyone else. He really was a good guy, just had some bad habits and none of the finer graces. If that's what they were. He wasn't charming, but he was what he was.

She tried to find a way to thank him for the evening, but she just couldn't bring herself to do it. She kind of wished she'd just stayed home and spent a final few hours with her horses.

I have a responsibility that I'm going to need to take on, and I'm not going to have time to go out with you anymore. Thank you for the time that we spent together.

There. She thanked him for that. Which she felt was stretching it just a bit, because... She kind of felt like it was mostly wasted time. Even though he assuaged her ego at times.

Leaving the check where he would be sure to see it, she took one last look at Rick, leaning back between the door and the seat, tilted toward her just a little, his head back, his mouth wide open, snores that would wake the dead coming out of his mouth, his hands limp at his sides. A half-drunk beer in the cupholder beside him.

She wasn't going to miss him, and she wasn't sad about this. She never should have started anything, and she should have broken up long ago. If that's what this was.

Yanking on the handle, she hopped out, slid down the rail, and reached out to close the door behind her. It felt like she was closing it on a part of her life that she really didn't want to look back on at all. Those memories could sink down a black hole and disappear for all she cared.

Seven

"Welcome to the Blueberry Beach diner. Can I get you something to drink?" the waitress asked as Rodney sat at the corner booth, watching for Becky to come in the door.

"I'm waiting for someone, thank you. I'll order with her."

"Gotcha, darling." The waitress winked and then walked off.

He didn't want to stare but turned his head back out toward the street. Typically, Becky had always been early. In fact, she had given him a hard time more than once for being just a couple of minutes late.

She had driven that into him more than his own mother had, and he'd ended up being very punctual, early even, as a businessman. It was a habit that had paid him a lot of dividends over the years. Other people couldn't stick to deadlines, but he had Becky in the back of his head, urging him on, and he had to say, he never missed a meeting and had never been late to one.

And yet here he was, it was 2:11, and she still wasn't here.

And then the thought struck him. She was going to stand him up. She was going to do that to get back at him for ghosting her five years ago.

Really? He couldn't believe that of Becky. Especially since they were meeting to talk about her sister's kids. There wasn't anyone in the world

43

who meant more to her than her sister did, and the idea that she would stick it to him, just to get back at him, and throw her sister and her kids underneath the bus...that wasn't the Becky he knew.

But people changed.

He got his phone out and set it on the table. At 2:20, he would leave. He had her old number, but he'd tried it after her sister had called him, and it hadn't worked. That's why he had ended up going to see her. He supposed he knew people who'd probably have her new number, but he was annoyed, and he wasn't going to try to find it.

If she blew him off, she could find him. That's the way he felt about that. He would show up on Friday, because he promised Rita, but if Becky wanted to deal with him, she could track him down at the hospital, and they could do it then. He didn't care.

At 2:20, he admitted that Becky wasn't who he thought she was, or she changed a lot anyway. He threw some money down on the table for a tip for the waitress. She'd brought him ice water, even though he'd not requested anything, and he figured he owed her something for her time. Plus, one of the things that Davis and Matt and especially Ford Hansen had drummed into his brain was that when a person had money, that made them more generous, not less. It was always better to be generous. And all of those men, at one time or another, had quoted Luke 6:38:

> **Give, and it shall be given unto you; good measure,**
> **pressed down, and shaken together, and**
> **running over, shall men give into your bosom.**
> **For with the same measure that ye mete withal**
> **it shall be measured to you again.**

As he thought about that, he stopped, walked back to the table, and put a one-hundred-dollar bill down. There. Hopefully that would make someone's day.

He turned around and walked out. Disappointed. Disappointed in himself for what he had ruined with Becky years ago. Disappointed with Becky for not showing up, for not being the person he thought she was, for jumping to assumptions about him, not giving him a chance to explain. And most of all, for blowing off her sister and her babies. For not keeping her word when she agreed to meet with him, for not trying to figure out a solution that would be best for both of them. Instead, the babies were going to be born, and they were not going to have any kind of plan in place for them.

He stomped off down the sidewalk, wishing he hadn't driven the whole way back from Chicago just to face an empty diner, just to drive back to Chicago to finish up what he needed to do before he went to the hospital on Friday.

Still, there was a part of his heart that hurt. Because...he loved Becky. Loved the girl she had been anyway, the woman she had become, and... maybe the person she was now. He wanted to love her. To him, love wasn't just a feeling, it was kind, it was not prideful, it was patient.

And there he was, he'd given her twenty minutes and no more.

He shoved his hands in his pockets and stopped right beside his SUV.

Should he have given her more time?

He pressed his lips together. He doubted it. People didn't show up twenty minutes late. Especially Becky. She wasn't coming. So why was he feeling so guilty that he wasn't patient?

Maybe he was jumping to conclusions about who she was.

He wasn't sure, he just knew she was supposed to be there and she wasn't, and he felt like it was on purpose, a slam against him for whatever reason. Whether to get him back, or whether she was just flat-out mad.

He probably deserved it though. After the way he treated her, who was he to be upset with her?

He knew that was the right way to think about it as he walked in front of his vehicle. The locks clicked as he got close to the driver-side door and then got in.

He needed to be humble. If he saw Becky at the hospital, he would not be angry, he would be kind. Because... She deserved his kindness. After the way he treated her anyway, and as a Christian, that was who he wanted to be. No matter how people treated him.

Eight

Becky opened her hand and slapped the side of her pickup.

Of all the days for her pickup to decide to not start, today was the day. This was just great. She had to get feed, her horses were going to starve, and she was supposed to be meeting with Rodney in...she pulled her phone out of her pocket. Five minutes ago. She was supposed to be there five minutes ago.

She'd spent the last twenty minutes trying to get her stupid truck started, and of course, it wouldn't start today. Of course, today was the coldest day of the year so far, with a low of -21 this morning.

The water in the barn had frozen, and her toilet had ice chunks floating in it before she flushed it.

She'd actually clicked the heat up a few notches, even though she had no idea where she was going to get the money to pay for it.

She stood beside her truck, her eyes closed, her head back, lifting her face to the Lord, silently asking for help.

But God was quiet about what she should do about her truck.

She knew what she needed to do about her horses though. She decided that she would at least do it in the relative warmth of her apartment. It was warmer than it usually was, and she was already shivering, despite her frustration and anger.

If she had a can of ether, she might have been able to get her truck started, but she couldn't spray the ether and turn it over at the same time, so she still had to take the time to go get someone to help her, and by then, Rodney absolutely would not be waiting around for her.

Not that he didn't deserve her standing him up, but she wouldn't have done it. He would have known that she wouldn't have done it, of course. He probably wondered where she was. In fact, she wouldn't be the slightest bit surprised if he came out to check on her. After all, he knew she got angry, but he also knew that she was fair, and honest, and very, very punctual.

She did not smile, although she did remember a few times giving him a long, passionate lecture about how it was important for responsible people to be on time.

She made it into the house, and up the stairs, and sat down in the folding chair that made up her entire kitchen seating arrangements. After pulling her gloves off, she got her phone out. She'd been composing the ad in her head for some time now, and so the words flowed easily from her fingers.

She knew that she could price her horses to sell, and they would be gone in hours. What she had was high quality, and they were well trained and had absolutely no vices.

She could command top dollar for them, but she was willing to take about eighty percent of what they were worth, just to get them sold quickly. She didn't want to drag this on any longer. The sooner she got rid of them, the sooner she would have to stop buying feed, and...if she got rid of them tomorrow, it wouldn't matter that she'd run out of feed tonight.

She still had hay, and they'd be okay without grain for once.

By the time she was done and hit post, tears streamed down her face, and she was glad she had chosen to do it in the warmth of her apartment. They would have been frozen if she would have been sitting downstairs in the stable. And how could she sit in the stable with the horses of her heart when she knew she was posting them to sell?

They might not go together either. She hadn't specified in her post that they needed to. She would split them up if she had to, and they would be fine. No one was going to pay what she was asking for these horses and not take good care of them. But still, she would vet their homes, and in the ad, she required references.

There. That hard thing was done. She'd broken up with Rick, if one could call it that, and now, all she had to do was get a reliable vehicle. Because if she was going to have babies, she was going to have to take them to doctor's appointments at least, and she needed something that she could get around in.

She would trade her truck in for a little car. One that was big enough to have car seats in the back and a trunk that could haul whatever paraphernalia babies required. She was pretty sure it was a good bit. She'd been around enough babies in her life to know that kids could be rather high maintenance at times.

Her heart ached, but her chest felt lighter. She knew she was doing the right thing. People were always more important than things. Even when she loved those things with all of her heart.

Lord, I know I'm doing the right thing. I just wish it didn't hurt so much.

Nine

"I know you thought I was going to lead this, but the situation has changed, and my friend, Ford Hansen, is going to be taking over."

There were murmurs around the room as Rodney stood at the head of the table. Ford wasn't at the meeting, and he wasn't videoing in either, but he had agreed to buy Rodney's share and take over Rodney's position.

Ford was one of the few men Rodney knew who could afford to do it. There was a huge payoff involved. It was what Rodney had been banking on to make him a billionaire in the next two years. Managed right, it would do just that for Ford.

Ford had not been doing him a favor by buying him out. Rodney had been doing him a favor by asking him.

But the fact remained that Rodney was now out from underneath seventy percent of the responsibilities that he had taken upon himself. The other thirty percent were easily manageable. It wasn't how he had seen his life playing out, but if he was going to take on the responsibility for twin babies, for who knew how long, he hadn't had a choice. Unless he was going to hire someone to take care of the babies for him.

Plenty of people hired out childcare, and if he were talking about forty hours a week, he might have considered it. But he was going to need a full-time nanny, because one didn't get to the level that he was in with his business by working just forty hours a week.

He finished out the meeting, answering the questions that were inevitable when they were talking about a shift that size. It was almost unheard of, but he and Ford could make it work. They always did. They worked well together, and Ford had been invaluable to him. Again, he hadn't saved him when Rodney had made some really terrible decisions, and in hindsight, Rodney was exceptionally glad that Ford had stepped back and allowed things to unfold the way they needed to. The lessons he learned had been invaluable. He couldn't have learned them any other way.

Not that he didn't wish that it wouldn't have happened. Because... his relationship with Becky would have been a lot better. But that was his own fault too. Another bad decision that didn't have to be. He could have told her everything, he could have kept her in the loop, and he could have saved that relationship.

But he'd been stubborn and stupid, and he hadn't listened to his mentors when they had told him to just be honest and tell her what happened.

He had been too proud to.

Well, he wasn't too proud to sell off when he knew that that's what he needed to do. And he wasn't too proud to apologize to Becky, even though she stood him up on Wednesday.

He was annoyed, but he realized that was just a small part of how she felt five years ago when he had stopped responding to her at all. He'd sent her letters back, and he changed his number. She hadn't been able to get a hold of him at all, since he'd lost his apartment. Even if she tried to look him up, she couldn't. He told everyone to not tell her anything. Whether she had gone and asked, he didn't even know. People didn't talk to him about it because he told them he was done. He wasn't going to talk to her again until he was a billionaire.

Well, he hadn't stuck to that, but that was because of Rita. If it hadn't been for Rita, he would still be on the road he was on and not realize how Becky had...been hurt? Changed? Maybe both.

He walked out of the boardroom and was stopped by Jordan, a longtime friend.

"What's going on? I couldn't ask in the meeting, but I was a little flabbergasted when this all went down. Are you okay?"

He looked both ways in the hall, and then he jerked his head. "Let's go to my office."

They walked past the rows of cubicles until they got to his glass-enclosed corner office.

There was a private bathroom inside and a beautiful view of the Chicago River.

He'd wished that the view had been of the lake, but...he hadn't gotten around to finding office space that gave him the view he wanted. The lake reminded him of Blueberry Beach, of Strawberry Sands and Raspberry Ridge and his friendship with Becky.

Maybe he hadn't wanted that, really. What he really wanted was to ditch his office and go home.

"Dude? What's up?" Jordan spoke as soon as the door clicked closed.

Rodney smiled reassuringly. "I'm fine. Everything's fine. Just...life changes sometimes, right?"

"It changes?" He lifted his brows in surprise, and then he narrowed his eyes. "Did Stella finally get a hold of you?"

"Stella?" Rodney asked.

"She's had a baby, and she's claiming it's yours. She told me she was going to get a child's ransom out of you, but...she needed to go to her lawyer or something."

Rodney felt his stomach dropping out. Stella had a baby?

He ran a hand through his hair, turned toward the window, and tried to think back. He couldn't have a baby with Stella, right? But four and a half years ago when he had been at his lowest point, unable to renew his lease because he couldn't make the payments, he'd been kicked out of his apartment, and Stella had offered to let him stay with her.

It had been a really bad decision on his part. One he thought he had overcome, because it had only been for a few months, because he'd gotten the cheapest apartment he could find in a rundown section of town, one no one had any business living in, and had moved out. Which had been easy. He'd had just three suits and a handful of T-shirts and jeans.

But still, Stella had only had a one-bedroom apartment, and...they could have a child together. But it wouldn't be a baby.

"Rodney? Hello?" Jordan waved a hand in front of Rodney's face. "Did you hear me?" He snorted. "I'm pretty sure you're not okay. I feel like I need to call an ambulance."

"No. Don't bother. I'm fine." He took a breath. "If Stella has a baby, it's not mine."

"She's claiming it is."

"How old?" Rodney asked, and Jordan's eyes changed. Just by that very question, he was admitting that there was a possibility.

"I didn't ask. I thought she said baby, but maybe she said kid. I don't know. I haven't seen Stella for several years, and maybe I just assumed that if she had a kid, it was a baby."

"I haven't seen Stella for years either. If it's a baby, it's not mine."

His voice was quiet and calm, but...inside, he was roiling. He'd made a huge mistake, which was part of the reason he'd moved out of Stella's place. It was his biggest regret and one he'd tried hard to forget.

This was definitely not what he expected on top of everything else. It was one thing to sell his businesses and give up the dream that he had been working toward. It was another thing to know that the woman that he had done everything for now wanted to have nothing to do with him. And quite another to have agreed to act as a father figure, with said woman who wanted nothing to do with him, to twin babies who were going to be born on Friday.

And now this.

"I feel like if Stella had your kid, she would have tried to get money out of you a long time ago."

"I feel that way too," he said. His heart was still racing, and his hands had started to sweat.

If Becky was mad at him for ghosting her five years ago, she was going to be...disappointed and disgusted if she heard about this.

He was disappointed and disgusted. He'd been disappointed and disgusted with himself at the time. And he'd never considered the possibility of a child. The idea that he'd had a son or daughter all this time that he'd not known about, who hadn't known he had a dad... That was even worse. But could it really be his?

Stella was not exactly virtuous, and a couple of times while he'd been there, she'd tiptoed past him while he slept on the couch and had one of her boyfriends sleep over. It was never the same one.

Regardless. It was done now, and he would have to face whatever he had to face. Whether that was the disappointment on Becky's face. Or if he thought his mentors were going to be disappointed about him not going after the billion dollars, they would be even more disappointed about that. All of them, to a man, had warned him about that.

And he'd listened. He'd listened up until that point. But he'd just been so low, and she'd been so kind and sweet and provocative...he had been no match for her, basically.

He still wasn't.

Still, he couldn't expect Becky to forgive that. She might have forgiven the indiscretion, because he would have confessed it, but to have a child? No, it would be impossible for Becky to forgive that.

Ten

"So that's why you're selling out?" Jordan said, bringing Rodney's focus back to the present.

"No. I didn't even know about that. But there are some other things. Nothing major, just life changes, you know? And Ford Hansen really, really wanted that deal. So, it didn't take much convincing on either of our parts to go through with it."

"I see," Jordan said, nodding. It really wasn't a satisfactory explanation, but it was all Jordan was going to get, and he seemed to realize that.

"Well, I'll see you around," Jordan said.

Rodney nodded and watched as his friend saw himself out.

He wasn't a drinking man, but he kind of wished he were right now, because he could use something to steady his nerves. He...wasn't expecting this turn of events.

Still, it was Thursday, and he wanted to go see Rita before she went to the hospital. She said she had to be there early in the morning. He hadn't questioned her too hard about it, but he wanted to go see her the night before, just because...he didn't know how the surgery was going to go, and he wasn't entirely sure he would ever be able to have a full conversation with her again.

He offered to meet her at a fancy restaurant, figuring he would take her out for a nice meal and treat her the way he wanted to treat Becky. After all, Becky loved Rita like she was her own daughter, and him being kind to Rita was basically him being kind to Becky.

She was the one who had his heart, after all.

Always had. From the time she broke into his bedroom and crawled into his bed.

The downtown traffic was terrible, rush hour and all that, and he was almost late for his meeting with Rita. Still, he arrived at the restaurant before she did, and stood outside, waiting on her. She texted him that she was going to be a few minutes, and while it was cold and the wind from the lake whipped down the street, he welcomed the uncomfortable feeling.

It helped cool some of the burning fire in his chest. The fire that came from the knowledge that he screwed up his life more than he thought.

Meeting with Rita, and helping her, would maybe make it right a little bit, but...he might have a child that he never met.

That made him angry. How dare Stella keep the child away from him?

But most of him thought that she was lying. Especially if it was a baby. Still, that child needed a father. Someone needed to step up and claim it. Or maybe Stella just wanted the richest guy to step up, even if she had to force him.

What if he didn't fight her? What if he just accepted the child and became a father to it?

He had no idea where that idea came from. That certainly wasn't on his radar. He wasn't interested in being a father to anyone's child except for Becky's, and being how infatuated she was with her horses, he used to wonder if she would ever want to have children. Her horses were her babies. They always had been.

And he'd seen those Clydesdales. They were her dream come true. He would be willing to bet that in the summer, she would be sleeping in the stable with her horses, rather than in her bed, just because she loved them that much. She'd probably do it in the winter too if she didn't think she'd freeze to death. A shot of fear went through him when he figured she was stubborn and gritty enough to attempt it anyway.

The crazy girl. It was amazing that she had made it this far in life without any kind of major catastrophe happening to her, as much as she rushed headlong into things, with a bulldog stubbornness that was absolutely unmatched.

He shouldn't have left her alone so long without his protection. Who knew what she could have gotten herself into.

And then he thought about himself and the possibility that he had a child, and he thought that maybe he was the one who shouldn't have been left alone.

Not that she had a choice.

"Hey there. My goodness, it's cold out," Rita said, walking up to him.

He had to do a double take. It had been a while since he had seen her, but he wouldn't have recognized her. Her eyes were sunken, her face sallow, her stomach sticking out, and the rest of her looked like a stick.

"I'm supposed to be on bed rest, but I was not going to say no to a fancy restaurant. I've never eaten here." She looked up at the big, shiny window and smiled an eager smile.

He had not realized she was on bed rest. "You should have told me you were on bed rest."

"And then we wouldn't be here, going to eat at a restaurant I never even knew existed. And can I say I am so excited? Although, I would feel bad if I didn't know you could afford it."

"Yeah. I can afford it. You don't need to feel bad. I also know people who know people, and while this restaurant usually does not do takeout, they would do it for me. We could have met at your bedside with the delicious food, and you would still be obeying your doctor's orders, and I would not feel terrified right now that something is going to happen and it's going to be my fault."

"Oh. I'm sorry. I didn't mean to terrify you," she said, not looking the slightest bit sorry. But she patted his arm and then nodded at the door. "Are we going in? I'm freezing."

She looked like it too. And he wondered if that was the sickness.

The cancer or whatever. She looked terrible. As she walked, she hunched over a little, as though she were in some kind of pain.

"Are you sure you're all right?" he said, leaning down so he could speak into her ear.

"I'm fine."

"You look like you're hurting."

"I am. But to eat here is worth it."

He could have told her that of all the places that he'd eaten, this was not the best. That the diner in Blueberry Beach had just as good food, and the atmosphere was much better. The company was even better than that. That here they would be eating with a bunch of people who thought that they were better than what they were and who looked down their noses on anyone who didn't have as much money or weren't what they considered sophisticated.

"Then let me escort you, my dear," he said, holding out his arm, which she looked at and then grinned up at him before tucking her arm in the crook of his elbow, grinning like she was on a date for prom.

If this was going to make her happy, then he was happy to do it. It was that verse about giving again. Sometimes giving wasn't necessarily money or things. Sometimes giving was time or an experience that another person couldn't have on their own.

The host found their reservation and then instructed them to be taken to their seats. He'd asked for the best one in the house and expected to get it, since he'd made the reservation earlier in the week and had added a little bit of money to go along with his request. Typically the place was booked out for months.

It was interesting what wealth could do. How it could grease the wheels and make life easier and, some would say, better.

"Wow. This is so amazing," she said, looking around. "Better than pictures, for sure."

"Better than the video they have on Facebook too," he said.

"Yeah, much better than any I've seen. Wow. The ambience." She sighed.

"You should have told me that you wanted to eat at a fancy restaurant sometime. You know it wouldn't have been a problem."

"I also knew that you were not talking to my sister, and I wasn't sure if that was a family thing, or if that was just a Becky thing. And I was afraid to reach out and find out, until I absolutely had to."

Guilt surged through him, and he didn't even try to tamp it down. After all, he deserved that.

"I'm sorry. I owe Becky a huge apology. But I'm not sure she's going to stand still and listen to it for me."

"I'm not so sure either. She was...not very happy when I told her that I wanted the two of you to co-parent. She...got angry with me, which she hasn't done for a really long time, and it was right after I told her that I had cancer. So, you know how angry she was." Rita laughed like cancer was a funny thing.

"Why are you laughing? You have cancer." He wanted to shake her. Didn't she know this was serious?

"I know. But I have my two favorite people in the entire world taking care of my babies, and there's a part of me," she tilted her head and looked at the ceiling, as though she were thinking, "a big part of me, that thinks that the two of you are going to do a better job of raising my kids than I ever could. I find the Lord's timing interesting."

"Well, it might be even more interesting than you think, because I just found out before I came here that there might be another kid involved."

"What do you mean?" Her brows furrowed. "I know I'm just having twins."

"A long time ago, right after I quit talking to Becky, which, by the way, was because I had lost everything. As in, everything. And I owed money. I was in a hole I didn't know how I was ever going to get out of, and I just couldn't face her. But that's not part of the story really."

"Oh my goodness. I didn't know. Maybe you can't afford this." She looked like she was ready to get up and run out of the restaurant.

"I assure you, Rita. I can. And far, far more. If you can believe that. If I had two more years, I would have been a billionaire if things had gone well. I had no reason to think that I wouldn't be since things were going to go very, very well. But that's neither here nor there. The point is, I quit talking to Becky because I lost everything. I was embarrassed, and I didn't want her to see me at such a low point. I couldn't even afford the rent for my apartment. I lost my lease, got kicked out, and a woman took me in."

"Oh?"

"Yeah. So she's the one with the kid."

"Oh my goodness. You cheated on Becky!" Her eyes were wide, and she looked horrified, and again, she looked like she was ready to run out of the restaurant, only this time it was because of him.

If he thought her reaction was bad, it wasn't anything compared to what Becky's was going to be.

"I was easy to take advantage of, because I had zero experience with anyone except for Becky, and I've never even kissed her."

"Oh my goodness," Rita said, and her tone was completely different. Appalled in a different way.

He lifted his shoulder. He was used to that. It wasn't exactly normal. "But I had no place to stay, so I was staying at this woman's apartment. It was a one-bedroom. She...was not shy about the fact that I slept on the couch while different men came to spend the night..."

"She was a hooker!" Rita's eyes got extremely large, and she really did start to stand up.

He reached across the table and put his hand over hers. "No. She wasn't a hooker. I think that's just what people do nowadays. They hook up, and it doesn't necessarily have to be the same person, even on the same night, although Stella wasn't like that." He tilted his head. "At least not while I was there. But anyway, suffice it to say that I only stayed for a few months. I got my own apartment. It was a cheap, dumpy place, complete with rats and leaking pipes, and in the seediest part of town you can imagine. It was not safe for anyone to be living there, I guarantee it. But it got me out of a bad situation."

He didn't bother to tell Rita that he only slept with Stella three times. It was relative, and even once was too much. It was a breakdown of the character of the man he thought he was and the man he wanted to be. He was someone at that time that he didn't even know.

But he couldn't take it back. He could only try to build back better. Himself, and his business.

"I suppose it's better to live in a place like that than to be having sex with someone that you're not married to, and with someone who's not Becky most of all."

"Yeah. It was a low point in my life. The lowest I've ever been for sure. I...would have told Becky about it eventually, but apparently there's a kid involved."

Eleven

Why was Rodney telling Rita this? He hadn't wanted to burden her. "So, yeah. There might be three children." He paused. "Even if that kid is not mine, obviously it has a dad who doesn't want it."

"Obviously Stella is trying to get money out of you. And it sounds like you're just going to let her."

"What about the kid? He thinks his dad doesn't want him. Whether he's mine, or whether he's someone else's, can you imagine?"

"No. I can't. I couldn't imagine my children thinking I didn't want them. And I can't imagine not knowing for sure that the people that I give them to would sacrifice everything they had for their happiness. But I know you, and I know my sister, and I know both of you will move heaven and earth to do the right thing for my kids. That's why I asked you. And her."

Rita nodded her head, and she looked him right in the eye. And in that moment, it confirmed that what he had done earlier in the day was the absolute right thing. It might have been the end of his dreams of being a billionaire. But he had plenty of money, plenty of investments to support himself in a lavish, if not extravagant, lifestyle for the rest of his life and to raise as many children as he felt like.

"I know you're right about Becky. She's fiercely loyal and stubbornly determined, and she's got grit like no one else I've ever met. I pity the person who tries to do anything unkind to either one of your babies. She will fight to the death for them."

"She's a tigress, that's for sure," Rita said with tender affection. "She tried to raise me right, and I got a little stubborn on her, but if there's anything good in me, it's because of Jesus and Becky."

"You said that in the right order anyway, and I have to agree."

"I'm not under any illusions about who I owe." Rita smiled.

"So tell me, what's really going on with you? What's going to happen tomorrow? How long do you think Becky and I are truly going to have these children?" It wasn't that he minded, he just really wanted to know what was going on with Rita. She had such a great attitude and a sense of humor that he admired, but that contrasted sharply with the color of her skin and how unhealthy she looked.

"All right. I'll level with you. They found something four months ago, but I wouldn't let them check it out any more, because I wasn't going to do anything that would harm the babies. They warned me that it could be a fast-growing cancer, because that was their suspicion, but I held firm. You know the treatment for cancer is not good for a person. Can you imagine what it would do to a baby?" She shuddered. "So, when I was close enough to my due date that they could do a C-section safely, I allowed them to do a biopsy." She forced a smile and tilted her head. "It's cancer. And I didn't mention this when we talked on Sunday, but it's the most aggressive kind. My prognosis is...poor."

"Poor? What does that mean?" he asked, feeling his leg start to shake up and down underneath the table. This was not looking good. Becky was going to be devastated. Not that he was happy about it. Becky loved her sister more than life.

"It means that, tomorrow, after they take the babies, they're going to try to operate on the tumor. They are afraid, though, that they're not going to be able to get it all, and they've given me a less than ten-percent chance, on a good day, when all the stars align and the planets do as well. I'm pretty sure that's a direct quote from the oncologist." She grinned, like it was funny.

"Holy smokes. Ten percent? To get all the tumor? Or to survive?"

"Yeah. I think I have like a seventy-percent chance of surviving the operation. But the ten-percent chance is my six-month survival prognosis." She looked at his shoulder. "The oncologist keeps saying that if I would have terminated the pregnancy, I might have been able to survive. But they don't understand, if I would have terminated the pregnancy, I wouldn't have wanted to live with myself after that. Who cares about the survival rates then? If I'm willing to kill defenseless human beings so that I can live? What kind of monster does that make me?" Her eyes were tortured at the thought. "Especially when you consider that those human beings are my own flesh and blood. No way."

Rodney sat and stared at Rita. He could see Becky so clearly in her. The grit, the determination, the absolute fortitude that it must have taken to make that decision in the face of all of her doctors pressuring her to do something different.

"I admire you. You...stood for something." Especially considering that they just spent the earlier part of their meal discussing how he had fallen for something stupid.

"Well, I was raised by the best." She grinned, giving a nod to her sister, Becky, that Rodney did not miss. He supposed Becky loomed large in Rita's life. She was a pretty strong figure for sure.

The rest of the meal passed in casual conversation, with Rita telling him that at first, she was assuming that they would take the children home to her apartment, and then once they found out whether the doctors could get all the cancer, and whether or not she would even go home, they would make some decisions from there. But everything was so up in the air that she really didn't know and couldn't make firm plans.

In the end, she said it was up to Becky and him as to what they wanted to do.

He couldn't see Becky going against what Rita wanted, but it wasn't firm, and maybe Becky would insist they separate the babies, and maybe each take one? Or maybe they'd split them by weeks or months or something. He could see Becky doing that. Although, from what Rita was saying, she was expecting them to raise them as a mom and dad, not as divorced parents who co-parented.

Still, unless Rita specifically said that, he was sure that Becky would take charge and make things work the way she wanted them to. Of course, she was going to want the best for the babies, and maybe she would get it in her head that the best thing for the babies would be for the two of them to parent together. He could only hope so.

Rita looked at her watch. "I have to stop eating at eight o'clock, and… I have five minutes to go." She looked at the last bite of cheesecake on her plate. "I just don't think I can hold it."

"I'd say I'd eat it for you, but I'm stuffed as well," Rodney said honestly. He'd eaten far too much, and all of it was really good.

"I'm a little disappointed though. I guess I can't say it's the best food I've ever had. But it's definitely the most interesting experience, luxury, you name it," Rita said as she looked around the room. Everything was black tie, serious, the food had been presented impeccably, and Rodney was so glad he could give her this experience. It hadn't even occurred to him that it might be something she would enjoy.

"I'm sorry you're disappointed with the food, but I guess I could have told you that you could get better food at the diner in Blueberry Beach."

"I agree," she said, laughing. "But the swankiness is unbeatable."

"Yes. You pay for the swankiness," he said.

"Hang on a second," she said as her phone buzzed. She looked at it, seemed to read a text, and then sent a quick reply back. "Becky's at my apartment. She has the code, and I told her to go ahead on in. She wanted to talk to me tonight too."

"You shouldn't be hungry while you're talking to her."

"And if I am, I can't eat. So, I'm glad you were agreeable to talking earlier." He couldn't get over how happy, almost bubbly, she was, despite how terrible she looked and the ordeal she was facing tomorrow and the possibility that she might not even survive the operation, let alone be here next year this time.

"Is there anything else I can do for you?" he asked.

"I… I know that things aren't great between you and Becky, and I just ask that you be patient with her. She's…well, you know, she's been through a lot. And she loves you. She always has. I don't know what she's saying now, but there is not any doubt that she loves you. I know she's with that jerk-face idiot who doesn't deserve to lick her feet—"

"Wait. What?" He blinked. Becky was with someone?

Rita snapped her mouth shut. And then she seemed confused. "Didn't you know?"

"No. The first time I talked to her in years was earlier this week when I went to the farm to see her, because I didn't have her number and I wanted to get together with her. She stood me up on Wednesday when we were supposed to meet at the Blueberry Beach diner, and I haven't talked to her since."

"She stood you up?" Rita's brows furrowed.

"Yeah. I don't want to go on about it, but we were supposed to meet, and she didn't show."

"Her truck probably wouldn't start." Rita seemed to be thoughtful. "Was it the day it was really cold?"

"It was really cold all week this week," he said, but then after thinking about it, he agreed. "I do think Wednesday was the coldest day."

"Yeah. Her stupid truck. I've told her over and over that she needs to get something newer, something that at least starts, but...she won't listen. She keeps insisting that she needs it for the horses and that trucks are too expensive for her to buy anything newer."

Becky was having trouble with money? He just assumed that she was fine. That Matt and Davis were taking care of her if there were any problems, but come to think about it, she was in Raspberry Ridge, and they both said they hadn't talked to her in a while.

"She's struggling?" he asked, wanting to jump up out of his chair and go help her immediately, which was ridiculous. First of all, she had stood him up earlier in the week, and second of all, he was going to see her the next day, when they met at the hospital for Rita's surgery.

"I don't think so. Although, I guess she must be a little bit, if she can't afford to buy a new truck. But you know how she gets attached to things," Rita said. "And when I asked her about the twins, she didn't say a word about not being able to afford them. You know she would have if she didn't think she could do a very good job. The very best."

"You're right. It just must be that she got attached to that stupid old thing and can't get rid of it when she knows she needs to."

Nothing else made sense.

"But if you don't mind, I called an Uber, and it's waiting for me now," Rita said as she looked back down at her phone.

"Sure." He had already taken care of the bill, and he stood, grabbing her coat from the back of her chair and helping her into it. It was the nastiest coat in the room, but it was on the body containing the most beautiful spirit there. Rita was a true beauty, inside and out, and he felt blessed to know her. She'd taken a life that wasn't the best and had cultivated an attitude that made people forget that she was going through something that was harder than most people ever dreamed of. And she did it with a smile and a laugh and questions about him and what he was going through, and she didn't focus on herself or complain the entire time. It was admirable.

He walked her out, helped her in the Uber, and watched as she drove away.

His mind went back to Becky, and he realized that Rita and he had never talked about this person that she was with. Was it serious? He supposed in five years it could have become that way. But he just couldn't believe that Becky would do that to him. She was so loyal and dependable. But...Matt and Davis had warned him. They had said that there was a downside to her loyalty, and that was the grudge that she carried. He'd seen it himself, but he just didn't ever think her love for him could flip into anything else.

He must have been wrong. This was going to complicate things. If Becky was with someone, it would complicate things as much as him having a child.

He couldn't even blame her for being with someone, especially if he came with a child. How could he give her a hard time, when he obviously wasn't faithful?

What a mess. He wanted to say that he couldn't believe what a mess his life had become, but that wouldn't have been true. This actually was very reminiscent of five years ago, when even then, he couldn't believe what a mess his life had become.

Tomorrow might be interesting. Of course, that was only if Becky was talking to him. In the meantime, he was going to go home, and he was going to pray as hard as he could for Rita and the babies and for Becky most of all. That there was some kind of spark, some kind of feeling left for him in her heart, and that whoever she was with wasn't someone she had feelings for. That it was just...someone she was putting in time with. Except, that wasn't Becky. She did everything with her whole heart and soul.

When he looked at it, it seemed hopeless, but he knew that God had worked huge miracles in his life, and God could work this out too. He just had to have faith that it would happen.

Twelve

"Rita!" Becky said, opening the door and enveloping her sister in a huge hug.

Her sister's heat was turned down too, although not as far as the heat in her little apartment above the barn was. Now, with the horses gone—they had left earlier that afternoon—she didn't need the water to not freeze. So she turned it completely off and shut the heat off as well.

If she had to go back to her apartment, she could turn the water back on, and it should be fine.

"Becky. I'm so glad you're here," Rita said, walking in and closing the door behind her. Becky was surprised to see her all dressed up.

"Well. You look like you've been at the opera or something," Becky said, standing back and looking at Rita in her long dress coat and beautiful ball gown-type dress.

"I picked this up at the Goodwill store. It was five dollars. It's got a hole in it right here," Rita said, shoving her finger through a hole in the side of the coat. "The shoes were a buck, and the dress was seven."

"So you were at the opera," Becky said, wondering where in the world Rita was. She was much less interested in where Rita got the outfit than that she actually was wearing it somewhere.

"No. I went out to eat with Rodney." She paused. "It was a fancy restaurant."

"Well. I'd say fancy. Rodney, huh?"

She tried not to look jealous. Was Rodney with Rita?

"Is that the father of your babies?" Becky couldn't stop herself from asking.

Rita jerked back, like Becky had slapped her. "No!" She took a deep breath before she continued. "No. Sorry. I guess that's a logical conclusion considering how little we talk. But I know what the plan is on your phone, and you said you try to be careful, so..."

"No. I'm not blaming you. Like you said, it was a logical conclusion."

"Yeah. No, that's not it at all. I told you who the father was, and that's who it is. And Rodney and I are not together. I just knew that you and he would be the two best people in the entire world to raise my children. And if anything happens to me, I wanted you to. He just wanted to talk to me. The same reason you're here early instead of showing up tomorrow at the hospital."

"Oh. Okay. That's nice. What's a fancy restaurant like?" Becky asked, having never been to a fancy restaurant. Rodney had told her that someday they would, but those had been more of the empty promises he'd made a lonely girl who was too in love with the boy to see that he was just lying to her.

"It was awesome. I mean, black ties, the waiter looking so serious," she said, lowering her voice a little and doing a little imitation of the waiter, "flipping his towel over his forearm. Everyone was so beautiful, but...it lacked soul, you know?"

"Okay." She could kind of see what Rita might be saying. "And the food?" Becky asked, the practical girl in her coming out.

"Oh my goodness. It was really, really good, but you can get food just as good at the diner in Blueberry Beach. In fact, I told Rodney that the food in Blueberry Beach is better."

"Well. That probably hurt his feelings, because I'm guessing that the meal was not cheap."

"No. It was not cheap. It was so expensive they didn't even put the prices on the menu." Rita lifted her eyebrows, just to show how shocking that was.

"I see."

"Do you mind if I change into something more comfortable? The dress is really pretty and made me feel beautiful tonight, but I'm exhausted."

She'd already kicked her shoes off, and Becky felt terrible for making her stand.

"Of course. And didn't you say that you were supposed to be on bed rest?"

"I promise, I spent the entire day in bed until it was time to get up and get ready to go. And I have every intention of going back there now. You don't mind talking to me while I lie down, do you?"

Becky almost gave her a hard time, because she sat up while she talked to Rodney, that she was going to lie down while she talked to Becky, but...that probably showed that she was a lot more comfortable with Becky than she was with Rodney and was more of a compliment than anything. Regardless, she wanted her sister to be comfortable, and she definitely did not want her to go into labor before she got to the hospital the next day. And certainly not with a full stomach.

She went into the bathroom, and when she came out, she was dressed in a T-shirt and comfortable yoga pants.

"All right, all I'm allowed to have from now until four AM is water. After that, I'm not even allowed to have that."

"All right. You want me to wake you up at four and make sure you take a drink?" Becky asked as Rita walked to her bed.

"If you don't mind, I'd love it if you would do that. I can set my alarm, but sometimes I sleep through it. And then sometimes I can't sleep for anything."

"I've heard pregnancy is hard like that."

"Yeah. I've heard that twins is even harder."

Rita looked terrible. Her eyes were sunken in black rims, and out of the dress, she looked pathetically skinny, except for the huge ball in her stomach.

It looked like she was putting all of her energy into making the babies and none into taking care of herself.

"I just want to go over some things that you need me to do. I mean, what are you expecting?"

"The only thing I expect is for you and Rodney to get along. I want you to parent the babies together as much as possible. I know you have your horses and he has his business, and you might not have time, but... I don't want you guys fighting."

Becky looked down. First of all, she didn't have horses anymore. She fingered the eye drops in her pocket. She had cried for two hours after they'd left at one o'clock. Then, she turned the water off, drained the lines, turned heat off, and put eye drops in her eyes before she packed a few clothes and headed toward Blueberry Beach. The people who had bought the horses had wired the money the day before, and that morning, Becky had gone to the used car dealership and traded her old truck on a car that was supposed to be guaranteed to start for six months. She figured that Rita should be better by then or at least well enough to be taking care of the babies again, and that's what she needed. A six-month guarantee that the car wouldn't leave her sitting beside the road with newborns in the back.

Regardless, it had started like promised and had brought her to Chicago.

It was not her Clydesdale horses, but...it was what she needed in order to be the sister that she wanted to be. She couldn't be the person she wanted to be without making the sacrifices that were necessary to be that person. Even she, amid her muddled-up, mistake-ridden life, knew that.

Regardless, Rita would not know that she had been crying. She brought the eye drops along just in case she got hit with another crying spell at any point. Hopefully by now, if she cried, Rita would think it was for her.

And it very well might be.

"Are you gonna tell me about what's going on?"

Rita lay back, her eyes closed. "I had to have car seats in order for the babies to leave the hospital. So, maybe you saw them sitting on the floor in the kitchen. They're still in their boxes. I... I want to get that and clothes and monitors and bottles and all the things that you need for babies, but... I couldn't work for the last six weeks, and I needed the money to pay the rent on the apartment. I'm sorry." She opened her eyes and looked directly at Becky.

Becky wished that she had sold her horses two months ago. She would have, too, if Rita had told her what was going on.

"I don't understand why you kept this from me. It makes me angry, but I don't want to waste our last night together before your surgery fighting."

That was the only reason she wasn't yelling at her sister right now. Well, that, and in order to be the person she wanted to be, she had to make sacrifices that led her to become that person. Sacrifices like not yelling when she felt like it.

"Thank you. I appreciate that." Rita went on to explain that they might be taking the cancer out during the surgery and that there was a possibility that she might not wake up.

Becky gasped. "What?" This was not what she was expecting. From her phone call, she knew Rita had said cancer, but she thought she meant a little cancer, like, she didn't know, something on her finger or something.

No, she knew it was going to be more than that, but she was thinking breast cancer, like they just take the babies and a boob or two.

"Yeah. It's...a pretty big mass from what they can tell, but I wouldn't let them do any imaging that was going to hurt the babies. So, since I'm already going to be out, and they want to get it as quickly as possible, they're going to do whatever they need to do and then take as much as they can."

"All right. And then you're going to be better, right?" Becky couldn't help herself. She had her arms crossed over her chest as though to protect herself from all the hits that she was taking as she paced back and forth at the foot of the bed.

Becky hated it when she paced. Absolutely hated it, but she couldn't stop herself. This was way too much.

But no, actually it wasn't as much as what Rita had to say. By the time she was done, Becky needn't have worried about the eye drops in her pocket. She really was crying, and it wasn't for her horses. It was for her beautiful, brave sister who was facing the fight of her life and who had already admitted that most likely she was not going to win it.

"So now you see why I needed you. And Rodney. What better people to raise my babies than the two of you? I know that both of you will sacrifice whatever is necessary for their good and their welfare. And I know that you will do whatever I ask, so when I say that my one request is that you and Rodney get along and raise the babies together, I know you'll do it."

Rita sounded tired, but she also sounded shockingly cheerful, while Becky could not stop the tears from flowing out of her eyes, although she slapped them away as soon as they hit her cheeks.

"You're not going to just give up like that. I will not allow it." She knew she had her older sister's voice out in full force, and perhaps she was slightly more shrill than what she wanted to be. But this was an exceptional case.

"I'm sorry. But you don't get to make that call. God does. And I don't know what He's going to decide, but... I just have to accept it. And so do you."

"That doesn't mean you can't fight the cancer!" Becky practically screamed.

She needed to calm down. She needed to take deep breaths, just chill. Rita was not being deliberately obtuse, and she needed a cheerleader in her corner. "I will fight it for you."

"You are going to be raising my babies. With Rodney. I'll deal with the cancer."

"I don't even think we ought to say the C word. It's like giving it credence or something."

That made Rita laugh. Becky had not been joking. "I needed that. You're yelling at me, and I feel like I'm about three years old again."

"Sorry. I just..." Becky walked over and knelt beside the bed, clasping Rita's hand in hers. It was cold, and it made Becky want to get her up immediately and take her straight to the hospital. Should her hands be this cold?

"I know. And it's really not fair. I went through a period of denial and anger and sadness and, I don't know, just frustration with God for putting me through this. Why me? And then, I thought, why not me, right?"

Becky didn't want to agree, but it was true. She could ask why not just as much as she could ask why? And the questions were both equally legitimate. She couldn't really ask one without the other.

"Anyway. I've had time to process it. I've had time to accept it. I've had time to think about God's sovereignty in my life and how this is not something that I can change. So therefore, I'm going to surrender to God's will, fight what I can, but accept what I can't change. It's as simple as that."

"I don't know if it's that simple," Becky said softly.

"It is that simple. You can't change a thing, so why fight it? Just accept it, and you'll be a lot happier."

"Happiness is not my goal right now. Getting you better is."

"Raising my babies is your goal," Rita said, her voice stern, her eyes raised, meeting Becky's eyes and expecting her sister to nod in agreement.

"All right. Raising your babies is my goal. But getting you healthy is my goal as well. People can have more than one goal."

"You have two. Two babies. Two goals. You're taking care of both of them. You know, it's a boy and a girl."

"Oh my goodness, I never even thought to ask. Do you have names?"

"I sure do. Marley for the little girl, and Kevin for the boy. I'm not naming him after the father."

"I love them. They're perfect."

"And they might be just as close as adults as they are as children, but these two babies are going to be brother and sister. They're not any more the same than if I would have had them years apart. Except they're sharing my womb, and they'll be born at the same time."

"And they'll do everything together," Becky said, and then she thought... There was a boy and a girl, Rodney could have the boy, she could have a girl, and they wouldn't even need to know that they had siblings.

"I can tell that you're scheming. Stop it right now. You're not getting out of this. You promised." Rita did not sound desperate, but Becky got the impression that she actually was.

"Do Mom and Dad know about this?" Her sister would know she was referring to Luke and Kristen, the couple who had adopted them.

Currently Luke and Kristen were with Griff and Chi, the couple who had been instrumental in Rodney's life after his parents' horrible murder/suicide, sharing a cabin in the wilds of Alaska, a life-long bucket list item for both men.

"No. And they better not find out. If they have to come home early, after they've spent years saving and looking forward to this trip, because you told them about me, I will never forgive you. They've done way too much for us for us to even consider doing anything that would ruin this. Plus, the weather has been too bad for their weekly phone call for the last month. I haven't talked to them since Thanksgiving. I couldn't have told them if I wanted to."

Becky was quiet. Luke and Kristen would be upset that they hadn't been told, but they would understand. They'd been the absolutely best parents anyone could ask for and had supported Rita and Becky every way they could. Both Rita and Becky had been very careful to not take advantage of them, much to Luke and Kristen's consternation. They would do everything for their adoptive daughters if they could.

"Please, Becky. You know what it was like for us before Luke and Kristen. And you know even more than I do what it was like to feel like we didn't belong in the foster homes we were in. I want my babies to have a mom and a dad and be normal. To be raised the way babies are supposed to be raised, not shuttled back and forth without any kind of grounding whatsoever until they're teens, like we were."

"I told you I would do it. I meant I would. I'm not going to go back on my word. You know I wouldn't."

"Rodney told me that you were supposed to meet him on Wednesday at the diner in Blueberry Beach. He said you didn't show."

Becky's eyes got wide, and she looked at the hand she held. It was thin and translucent. She didn't want to talk to her sister about Rodney, about the pain she felt. Her sister already knew some of it, but maybe she didn't know the depths, and right now, Rita had enough on her plate.

"My truck wouldn't start. That's why there is a car in your driveway. I decided that I needed a reliable vehicle, so I traded my truck and got a car." She did not mention that she had to sell her horses in order to do that. That she looked at the price of formula and decided that she might as well just sell all four of them, because she was going to need that money and then somehow figure out how to make an income in order to continue to buy whatever the kids needed.

"Oh. I thought there was a car in the driveway, but in the excitement of seeing you and thinking about how tired I was and how much my feet hurt, I guess it just slipped my mind." She snorted. And then laughed. "I can't believe you got rid of that old clunker. Wow. You're moving up in the world!"

Becky wasn't sure that she was moving anywhere. The car wasn't really that much of an improvement over her old truck. It just had a six-month guarantee, and if it didn't start, the car dealer would come help her with it. For free. But Rita didn't need to know all of that.

Although, a six-month guarantee might not be long enough. If what Rita was saying was true, it was possible that in six months, she wouldn't have a sister.

"I just need you to get better, okay? I can't live without you."

"God promises to give you everything you need. If you have me, it's because you need me. And if He takes me, it's because you don't."

When did her sister get to be so wise, Becky wondered as she looked at her. Is that what happened when a person faced death and did it the right way? All of a sudden, the pieces of life fit into place, and they saw eternity through eyes that had wisdom beyond the years they'd lived?

Becky wasn't entirely sure, but one thing she did know, she didn't like to hear her sister talking like that.

"All right. So there are car seats. I'm going to need to buy bottles and formula and pack 'n plays or cribs or something. You have a list?" She had not researched babies. She had no idea what all they needed. But judging from Vera's house, they needed a lot. There was a ton of stuff that Vera claimed was nonnegotiable and absolutely essential. Even when they didn't have babies in their house, the stuff was ready so that if a foster child was available, they could get it immediately. It was a lot of stuff.

"I started one, but it's long, and I don't think it's everything." Rita waved a hand at her nightstand. "It's in the drawer there. Along with the pen. If you want, I can go over the stuff, but... I might fall asleep."

"No. Don't you worry about it. We'll go over it tomorrow while you're waiting for surgery. Or we'll go over it after you wake up."

"All right," Rita said, not mentioning that she might not wake up. A good thing because Becky was going to explode all over her if she even tried to say anything. She was not going to allow her sister to think anything but positive thoughts. She was going to survive the surgery, she was going to wake up, she was going to be around to raise her children. And that was that.

Thirteen

odney glanced at his watch after parking his car in the parking garage at the hospital.

He tried to look around and make sure he knew where he was. He hated these things. More often than not, he was thinking about where he was going and couldn't even remember what level he was on, let alone what space he was in. There should be some way of the ticket containing that information.

Thinking about that, he grabbed the pen out of his pocket and wrote the information down. That way, he would know. He wasn't sure how long he was going to be here. Just today? Would he stay with the twins? Would he go home and come back?

But the thing that he was most thinking about was Becky. He was going to see Becky. Any minute. Possibly she could be walking in right now. Although, he was guessing that she had taken her sister into surgery, and she would have needed to be there an hour or two early. The surgery wasn't scheduled until eight o'clock, and Rita had told Rodney that if he was there at 6:30, he should be able to see her before she went in.

They had promised that the babies would be available for them to see almost immediately after they were delivered, although the nurses and doctors would want to check them out.

Still, they knew what was going on, that Becky and Rodney were the de facto parents, and maybe it was because of Rita's cancer, but they were giving them parental rights.

They would need to check in with the nurses' station, but Rita had given Rodney all the information he needed.

He was early, thanks to Becky. He almost smiled, but he was too nervous.

Why was he nervous? He'd seen her on Monday. It wasn't like this was the first time he'd seen her for years and years or anything.

He reached deep, going to the place where he went when he had an important business meeting. One where the future hinged on it, and he needed to succeed, sometimes against all odds.

He had been pretty good at being calm in high-pressure situations. But they didn't include Becky. And she was more important than any business meeting. She was more important than billions of dollars; she was more important than anything.

He just hadn't realized it. Or maybe he realized it, just hadn't acted like it, and it was possible he lost her. That was where his nervousness was stemming from.

He walked into the hospital, following Rita's directions and showing his ID at the nurses' station. He got the proper credentials and was given directions to the surgical waiting room. They said that she had been prepped and moved to the last waiting point. Becky was with her. Normally they only allowed one person per patient, but because of Rita's unique situation, they were bending the rules just a bit.

He was going to see Becky.

He walked in, going to the third curtain, where he'd been directed. He looked again carefully, not wanting to pull the curtain on the wrong patient, and he saw Becky immediately.

In the bright lights of the hospital, with no heavy coat or hat on, she looked a lot different than she had on Monday.

First, he could see easily that her cheeks were much more sunken than they used to be. Her bones more prominent. Was that because she lost weight? Or because she'd matured beyond childhood and lost all the baby fat around her face?

He didn't remember her with any extra fat. She'd always been skinny. Partially because of neglect, and partially because she couldn't sit still for anything.

She was always into something, although the older she got, the more it was all good. He was the one who had struggled with the destructive habits and the sinful living.

But he never struggled with anything that had to do with relationships, because he wasn't willing to risk losing Becky.

Even though they were never together. He was much too old for her, and that was part of the reason he left. He was too old to be with her, so he figured he might as well go and have Ford Hansen teach him. The problem was, the more time he spent earning money, the more time he wanted to spend. The more he desired to earn more and more and what he had wasn't enough.

He could see now it was a vicious cycle. An addiction of sorts.

Second, Becky looked older today. Her hair was longer and darker than he remembered. Maybe it was darker because of the winter. Still, her fingers clasped the hand of her sister. Rita's eyes were closed, and she lay on the pillows, a tiny spot with a big bump right in the middle.

It looked like a peaceful scene. No one was fighting or throwing anything, and he wasn't entirely sure that would be the case once Becky saw that he was there.

She looked calm now, but he knew she was a spitfire and an absolute tigress when she knew she was right.

In this instance, she was right. About everything.

He moved the curtain and stepped into the room.

"Good morning, ladies," he said in his best and most charming voice.

Becky's lips pressed closed, but then she shot a glance at her sister, and something that resembled a smile came over her face.

"Good morning, Rodney. It was nice of you to come." She sounded sincere. He wasn't expecting sincere. He wasn't expecting her to be nice to him at all. Maybe that was what made the next words come out of his mouth.

"Yeah. I show up when I say I will." He used the same, charming tone. But his words were obviously not kind or charming.

Why would he do that? Becky was being nice to him. And he didn't want to fight in front of Rita. He didn't want to fight at all. Yet with his words, he just said he did.

What was wrong with him?

"Becky told me her truck wouldn't start. She traded it in on a car." Rita's words were slightly slurred.

"They gave her something to calm her," Becky said softly.

"Why did you tell him that?" Rita said, and she didn't sound like the happy, cheerful woman he'd met for supper last night.

Whatever it was had altered her personality. He didn't like that, but he went around to the other side and pulled the chair closer.

Was it true? Had Becky really not been able to get there?

He almost told her that she could have texted him and let him know, but then he remembered that he changed his number. She had no way of getting a hold of him.

"I'm sorry. I didn't know," he said, sincere.

But he could tell from her expression that his apology wasn't what she wanted to hear. Or maybe it just didn't matter. Still, her words were kind. "Of course. No problem."

"Maybe we should exchange phone numbers now, because...if I would have had your number, I would have tried to contact you."

He could tell from her expression that she wanted to deny him. To tell him that there was no need for him to have her number at all, but she did not. Instead, it was like she stretched her lips and made them settle into a smile.

"Of course. Whenever you're ready."

This was not the Becky he knew. This person was fake and only being kind because she had to. Was this the way they were going to parent together?

He supposed that he wouldn't mind. Just being around her was...so nice. It was so nice to be with her again. He just wanted to breathe in her presence. But he made a mess out of everything, and he owed her a huge explanation. Not just about the fact that he ghosted her, blocked her, and ignored her for five years, but also about the fact that there might be a child that he fathered with someone else.

Who was he kidding? Becky would never take him now. Not after the five-year freezeout, along with the baby. Obviously, he hadn't exorcised women from his life, just Becky.

She wasn't going to understand. He might as well not even try.

He had gotten his phone out and nodded his head. She rattled off her number, and he typed it into his phone, putting Becky with a heart into his contacts.

It was silly and juvenile of him, but... Even after all this time, even after everything, he still loved her. He could understand if she didn't love him. He deserved that, but he still loved her. He loved her fierceness, and her tenacity, and even the way she was acting right now, where she would do anything for her sister, even be kind to the man she hated.

Her phone buzzed as he sent her a text. It was just a "hi." He almost sent a heart, but she just would have been mad about it, and she wouldn't have understood that it was a heart that came from his heart.

At least, he knew her really well. As well as someone could know someone five years ago.

"All right, Rita. They're ready for you. Go ahead and hug your loved ones goodbye. As we mentioned, we have an observation window where they can watch. They'll be able to see the babies born. The doctors will hold them up, but then we're going to close the window, because the cancer surgery will begin."

"Okay, I got that. When will we be able to see Rita again?" Becky gripped Rita's hand in hers and stared at the nurse like she was a warrior in an enemy army.

"I'm sorry. I'm not sure. And the doctors themselves don't know. We haven't been able to do the tests we need to do because of the babies. But I can tell you that you should be able to hold the babies within an hour of their arrival. The doctors will look them over, the nurses will clean them up, and if they need to be warmed, they'll be under some lights. But we'll make sure that you two are as involved as possible. Okay?" The nurse was cheerful and perky and way too happy for that hour of the morning and for Rodney's mood in general, but he didn't need to let the blackness in his heart ruin her day, so he smiled and nodded.

Becky must have figured the same thing, because she smiled and said thank you as well. Then, she got up and hugged her sister. She whispered something in her sister's ear that made her sister laugh, but Rodney noted that when Becky stood, there were tears in her eyes.

He leaned over and hugged Rita as well. He wished he had something fun or funny or cute to say, but he didn't have anything other than, "I'm praying for you. I'm going to see you later." He made it sound like he meant every word. But there was an expression on the nurse's face that made him think that maybe he was dead wrong.

"All right, you two. You can follow me, and I'll point down the hall to where you can go. Someone will get you as soon as she's prepped and ready."

"All right," Becky said, and she sounded as uncertain as she had all day. He wanted to put an arm around her. Wanted to give her his strength and draw from her. Two people were far stronger than one. It wasn't a matter of one plus one. It was a multiplication that went on when two people were together. Ford had talked a little bit about that. Mostly in terms of business, but a couple of times when Ford's wife had been in the room, he could see it in Ford's relationship. Ford was more than the sum of the two of them. Ford was a multiplication of the two of them somehow.

That was not going to be Becky and him. In order to multiply, two people had to like each other and work together, and right now, he and Becky repelled each other.

Actually, it was him repelling Becky. Becky was doing no such thing to him. He was just as attracted to her as he had always been. Just as intrigued, just as pulled. It was an effort to try to move away from her.

Still, before he knew it, Rita was gone, and he and Becky were standing awkwardly together in the hall.

"I'm sorry you missed the meeting on Wednesday."

"Yeah," Becky said. Sounding preoccupied, like she was still thinking about her sister. But maybe she felt his eyes on her because she seemed to shake herself out of it and was the back-to-business Becky that he knew. "All right. Rita gave me a list of the things that she had ready for the babies. It's basically two car seats, and that's it. She has a list of the things that she needs, and it's pretty much everything. I tried to go over it with her this morning, and she really wasn't thinking very well at all. I... I tried to look online in several different places to get this figured out. What we need immediately, and what can wait. I have no experience in this, and I'm assuming you don't either?" She lifted her brows at him, although her eyes stopped about the height of his throat and didn't quite meet his gaze.

If he wanted to start things out right, despite the fact that it would be a total subject change, it was the right time to tell her that he had a child. But he didn't really know it for sure, and he couldn't get the words to come out.

As though the very thought conjured it up, his phone chimed, and without answering Becky, he looked down. It was his lawyer. He didn't read the whole text, just what came up on the notification.

> Sorry to bother you this early, but it's an emergency.

He didn't need to read any more. It could be a business emergency, or it could be an emergency as in Stella's lawyer reaching out and letting his lawyer know that he had a child and she was filing a paternity lawsuit.

"No. I have no experience," he finally said. He didn't need to make things harder. He would work on at least winning back her friendship before he confessed all the sins of his past.

There weren't that many, but there was one big one. And that was enough.

"All right. I don't either." Was that relief on her face? Had she wondered if he was with someone else? How he wished he had a completely clean slate and he could tell her that he'd never loved anyone but her. It was the truth, but...love didn't have anything to do with sex, at least that's what he found out with Stella.

He was ashamed to say it. Ashamed to think it, and it was all he could do to try to focus on what she was saying as she went through the list and talked about things that they needed to buy.

"I was in the process of trying to price things out and figure out what would be an even split. I guess, I could buy the bottles for Marley, and you could buy the bottles for Kevin—"

"Wait a second. Marley and Kevin?"

"That's what Rita wants to name them. It's a boy and a girl, and she wants to name them Marley and Kevin."

Wow. He hadn't even thought about names last night, and here was Becky, talking like she knew the babies already, and they hadn't even been born yet.

"The doctors are ready. Rita is prepped." The nurse appeared and motioned for them to go on down the hall. "You can stand here and look in the windows. You should be able to see the babies arrive and get some pics, but after they're taken, the curtains are going to shut. Don't panic. This is normal. That's what they're going to do, because they have more than just the babies to take care of."

"Got it," Becky said, and he murmured, "Thank you."

The nurse disappeared behind a door that clicked shut behind her.

They looked through the window where Rita lay on a table. There was a sheet between her head and her stomach, and Rodney assumed that that was so she couldn't see when they were cutting her open.

Then, he realized that her eyes were not open, and he wondered if they had put her out.

If he and Becky had a normal relationship, he might talk to her about it. As it was, he just stood, watching.

"Anyway. I was trying to figure out how to make it even. It seems silly for us to both go and buy the exact same things. But I want it to be fair."

"I'll buy everything. I'll pay for it, you shop for it. That's how we can split it."

He didn't mean to command it. He was just watching as the surgeon used some kind of sharp-looking things to pinch Rita's stomach, which looked extremely painful to Rodney, but Rita didn't move at all. Then, one of the assistants opened up a cloth-wrapped tray, and the surgeon picked up a scalpel.

"Does blood bother you?" he asked.

And then he realized that Becky hadn't responded to him.

He glanced down, and she seemed mesmerized as well.

"No. It never has."

He knew that about her. But the question had come out without him thinking about it. Blood did kind of bother him. He felt himself getting a little lightheaded.

He took a breath and looked away.

"Do you want me to ask for a seat for you? I do recall you passing out at least twice in biology class in high school."

So she remembered. Of course she did.

She didn't wait for him to respond but walked down to the nurses' station and asked if he could have a seat.

They seemed concerned, and there was a buzz of activity, but Becky being Becky, she came back with the chair and no extra nurses.

"Thanks," he said, sitting down. His eyes were just high enough for him to see through the window, and he felt a lot better now that he wasn't standing. Plus, the blood had been wiped away, and the surgeon seemed to be searching for something. A baby? The uterus? He wasn't sure.

"It's unfair that you pay and I shop. That's not equal."

"Parenting isn't equal. People do what their strengths are."

"Well, I'm not a strong shopper." Becky's voice held irritation. She didn't want to do the shopping.

"All right. You pay, I'll shop."

"I already said that's not fair." Her voice held more irritation and was slightly louder.

"If you're going to yell at me in this hallway, I am not going to talk to you. We are not going to have a fight right here in the hospital as our babies are being born."

She flinched when he said "our babies," and he almost smirked. There. Take that. Because they were going to be their babies.

And she knew he was right. It wouldn't be a good look for the two of them to be fighting in the hospital. They were supposed to be a loving couple getting ready to take care of the babies of a poor patient overcome by cancer. They were hardly poster people for parenting if they couldn't even get along long enough for the babies to be born.

"All right. What do you suggest?" he said when she didn't say anything.

The surgeon seemed to be pulling something out of a hole that looked way too small for anything human to fit through.

But the next thing he knew, the surgeon was holding up an infant in his hands, still connected by the umbilical cord, and then he turned around and held it up to the window. The surgeon was smiling, but the baby looked purple and wasn't breathing.

"I don't see the baby breathing," he said.

"Me either. The surgeon seems pretty happy. Surely he wouldn't be happy if he thought there was a problem, right?"

"Right. So this must be normal."

"Yeah. This is normal." Becky seemed to be trying to reassure herself of that, and him too, possibly, and then the surgeon turned back around, and they started working on the child.

"I think that was the girl," Becky murmured. "Marley."

He hadn't even noticed. Leave it to Becky to note something like that.

"So the girl's older. Interesting. I suppose they're timing this now."

"They must be," Becky said.

And then after a short pause, she said, "All right. I'll buy everything, you pay for it. I'll text you my info on several common electronic money transfer sites. You can take your pick which one you want to use."

"That's fair."

When she didn't reach for her phone, he said, "Aren't you gonna text me your info?"

"Right now? I'm watching the baby be born." And then she gasped. "I should have been recording it!"

"I see a nurse recording it over there. Maybe they're going to show it to us later."

"Oh. I didn't even see. You know what, now that you mention it, I think they did mention that a nurse would be recording if everything went well. If they were needed, they would throw their phone down, and we wouldn't get anything."

"I see."

"Yeah. Rita had to sign a consent form for it."

"Okay." He paused, somehow impatient to get her info. "I'm still waiting on that information." He wanted to send her money now. He had no idea of how much it was going to be, but this was the one area where he could absolutely take care of Becky. He didn't know whether he would be any good with babies. He had no idea what to do with them. But he did know he could pay for whatever she needed. Anything. Anything at all. And it would ease his mind to do that.

"I don't even know how much you need to send. Let me buy the stuff first."

But her voice lacked the usual Becky forcefulness, and it made him pause.

Did she have the money to buy it? Because of the tone of her voice, he almost thought the answer to that was most likely a no.

Interesting. He wasn't quite sure what to make of that, but he knew that he was going to dig a little deeper into it. Of course, he really didn't have the right, except Rita had forced them to be together and they needed to get along and figure this out. And maybe her financial situation was his business after all. Thanks to Rita.

"There's the other one," Becky said, and she didn't seem to be able to contain the excitement in her voice.

Sure enough, another tiny, tiny baby lay in the doctor's hands as he shifted it and then turned around and held it up so that they could see easily from the window.

"That's Kevin," Becky said, and he heard the tremor of excitement in her voice.

Or maybe that was a tremor of tears.

Because shortly after the surgeon turned around and they began to work on the baby, tying off the umbilical cord and doing whatever it was that they were doing, the curtain closed, and there was nothing to see.

"I guess we go back to the waiting room?" Rodney said, just as a nurse came out. The same one who had led them to the window to begin with.

"The waiting room is just down the hall on the left. You guys go there, and we'll give you any updates. Once the babies are washed and ready, we'll tell you you can come back and hold them, okay?" She lifted her brow but didn't wait for them to respond. She turned around and hurried right back inside the room.

"I guess that means we go and wait. Unless you have a better idea?"

Becky didn't move, and he wasn't sure if she thought she was going to stand there all day or what.

"No. I don't." She moved then, and they went to the waiting room.

There were two other men in the waiting room but no women. He assumed that maybe they were men whose wives were being operated on in some other operating room? He wasn't quite sure how many C-sections were done at one time. In fact, he really didn't know much of anything about the hospital except it was supposed to be a good one. It wasn't in the city, but sometimes that was just as well.

Now, it was Becky and him, and maybe if the men left, he would have some privacy to apologize. He felt like that's really where he needed to start. Even though Becky didn't seem open to any of that. That was what was on his chest.

Except then he remembered the text from his lawyer. It was before eight AM, and it really probably was an emergency.

"Do you mind if I leave for just a moment? I'll be right back," he said as they walked over to the seats, and Becky sat down.

"No," she said, waving her hand like she didn't give a flip what he did.

That hurt, but he figured he deserved it. He deserved everything she could do to him and more.

Walking out, he pulled up the full text. Just as he feared, it was his lawyer telling him that a paternity suit had been filed against him. He needed to call for the details. And to work out a strategy as to how they were going to fight it.

His lawyer assumed that he was going to fight it.

Blowing out a breath, he looked behind him to make sure the door was closed, and then just to be extra safe, he walked down the hall. He was going to tell Becky about this, but he didn't want to do it first. He wanted them to be friends at least. It wasn't that he was hiding things from her, he was just trying to...smooth their relationship over before he had to do something that...could shatter it completely.

It really shouldn't be that bad. If she didn't even like him, didn't even consider him a friend, far from thinking of him as any kind of romantic interest, then she probably wouldn't care who he was having children with, except this happened six months after he stopped talking to her. And he had known that there were at least three or four messages from her, begging him to talk to her, and letters that he had returned unopened.

She would assume that he was in this relationship and that was the reason why he wasn't talking to her. Instead of just telling her that he found someone else. Which of course he hadn't, but she wouldn't know and wouldn't understand.

He had pulled up his lawyer's contact, and the phone rang. It was his lawyer's cell phone, and he answered on the second ring.

"Rodney. You got my message?"

"I did. What's going on?"

"Some woman named Stella Coker has filed a suit alleging that her three-and-a-half-year-old son was fathered by you, and she wants money."

So, it wasn't a baby. The kid was the right age. On the one hand, his heart hurt, because he might have a son who thought he was unwanted. Who thought he didn't have a dad. Or who thought his dad was some deadbeat who went around making babies and then abandoning them.

Maybe all of that was true. But he hadn't done it intentionally. And he knew what the results of having sex were. It wasn't like he was naïve about that. At the time, he'd assumed that because Stella was with so many other men, she took precautions. He should have too. He'd thought about STDs after the fact, but it wasn't like he had ever done anything like that before, and he didn't have a stash of condoms.

He'd stopped before he became the kind of guy who did.

"Rodney. Why aren't you telling me that this woman couldn't possibly be the mother of your child?"

His lawyer knew he walked the straight and narrow. And he had probably been expecting an outright denial and anger at the idea that someone would be so bold.

"Because it could be true."

There was silence on the other end of the line. Finally his lawyer sighed, like he had to accept the inevitable. Or maybe like he was disappointed in Rodney. He couldn't possibly be more disappointed in Rodney than he was in himself.

"She claims she has a DNA test and the baby is definitely yours."

He wouldn't know how she would have been able to match his DNA, because he hadn't given her any. But he could understand why she would need one. He wasn't the only man she had slept with in the months he'd been there. Far from it.

"How much is she asking for?"

His lawyer relayed what the terms were, and they were in the millions. Of course.

Probably Stella hadn't realized that he was rich until just recently. She saw him as a meal ticket.

"Tell her I'll pay, but I want full custody of the child. Everything. She signs off."

Even as he said that, he felt bad. The child was probably attached to his mother, and that would upend his world. He didn't want to do that, but he also couldn't imagine Stella as a loving, caring mother. Just the fact that she was asking for millions told him that she was out for his money and not for the best interest of the child. Maybe he could be wrong.

"Am I allowed to get in touch with her?"

"No. Don't talk to her at all."

He pressed his lips together, not liking that answer but knowing that that was probably the way it needed to be.

"Do me a favor. Do some digging. Find out what she's like. Is she a good mom? Does she take care of him? Is he attached to her? Or is someone else watching him all the time?"

"I'm already on it. I assumed you were going to be fighting this. But regardless, I'll have that information and get it to you as soon as I get it."

"All right. Thanks."

He hung up. The call had put him into a black mood. It was...not ideal. The poor child. Whether he was the father or not, he didn't really care. He was going to get custody of him, and he was going to take care of him to the best of his ability. If he couldn't get custody, he was going to figure out what the very best thing for the child was, and then he was going to hire his lawyer to go full throttle after that. There was nothing that would stop him from doing the very best he could for that child. What was the point in having money if he didn't use it for good?

Fourteen

Becky sat in the waiting room, her whole body and soul tied up in knots. She twisted her hands together on her lap, and then when both of the men who had been sitting there walked out before Rodney came back, she got up and started to pace.

She was praying, but she wasn't casting her worry upon the Lord. She was holding it all tight to herself. It was pretty heavy.

Suddenly, she stopped pacing and thought.

Whatever happened, happened. Rita was at peace with it. Of that she was certain. So why wasn't she calm as well?

Maybe it was the idea that she didn't know whether or not she would be able to care for a baby, let alone two, and keep them alive. What did she know about children? She had loved horses all of her life and had spent all of her time learning about them. She hadn't paid the slightest bit of attention on how to raise a human.

She could learn. She'd learned plenty of things over her life. People had called her scrappy and determined. She was stubborn and gritty, and other people raised babies every day, she could too.

And she had Rodney.

She might not like him very much. At all. And he might have been a jerk to her, which was not an exaggeration. But he had always been dependable and smart and resourceful as well. He was also nurturing and caring. After all, he took care of her. When she was just a scrawny little rug rat who climbed in his bedroom at night, looking for things to eat.

He'd taken her in and fed her and cared for her and not turned her in. But made sure that she got directed to the right resources so that she would be cared for too.

Rodney might not have raised babies before, but he helped to raise her, and she had nothing but good memories about that. Just because he decided that he didn't love her in a romantic way was no reason for her to be mean. She didn't have to be unkind just because he had been unkind to her. She could be...nice.

She determined that she would. She would put everything he had done behind her. She would not hold it against him. She would forgive.

There. That was what she needed to do as a Christian anyway. That was what she had been resisting. That was what she had been hooked up on. Punishing Rodney. But her inability to forgive was punishing her. She was the one with the bitterness and anger that had been clutched close to her and all of those terrible things that it did to her insides.

Lord, I want to forgive Rodney. He hurt me. He really hurt me a lot, because I trusted him, and I don't trust too many people. You know that. He let me down. But why am I surprised? He's human, just like I am, and I've let plenty of people down and You, too, Lord. I've let You down. Help me to forgive Rodney. Forgive him for being human and for hurting me. Help me to love him the way You love him and to be kind to him.

Maybe her sister knew what she was doing after all. Maybe it was less about who she wanted to raise her babies and more about what she knew Becky needed in her life and soul.

The door opened. Rodney came in.

Now, she had a choice. She could smile and be nice, like she had just forgiven him, or she could continue to be a jerk back to him, because that's what he'd been to her.

He saw her look, and he paused, then continued in the room. His eyes held a bit of confusion, like he noticed a change in her but couldn't quite figure it out.

She took three steps forward and met him in the middle of the room, thankful the men had left.

"I've not been kind to you, and I'm sorry. You hurt me when you stopped talking to me and wouldn't take my calls and sent my letters back, and all of that." She waved her hand, indicating it was in the past. "And I was unkind because of the pain, and I guess I wanted to lash out at you. I'm sorry. I'm not going to do that anymore." She took a breath. "I forgive you."

He hadn't apologized. But he did not need to. He didn't need to ask for forgiveness in order for her to extend it. He could accept her forgiveness, or he could ignore it. That was up to him. For her, she felt so much better. Just lighter inside. Like she'd swept out the dark corners and gotten rid of the gunk that had been clogging up her soul.

Maybe she literally had.

He blinked. Obviously she'd surprised him. Then, he ran a hand through his hair, which was already standing on end, although it was short and cute. He always had a little bit of wave, and while it was too short for it to be lying in waves on his head, she could see the small tendency to curl, and she allowed herself to smile at it.

He shoved his phone in his pocket and then shifted. "I don't know where to start. I...don't really deserve your forgiveness. I haven't apologized properly."

"You don't need to. I really don't want you to."

"But may I, please? I've wanted to, but...it might take a while."

"Rodney Blackstone? Becky Rivers?" A nurse pushed open the door and called their names. She looked around the room and saw that they were the only two and they were staring at her. "Come with me. Your babies are ready."

Rodney gave her a look and then leaned down. "I do want to talk to you. Desperately."

She nodded and then took a step before she said, "I guess we'll be spending a lot of time together. I'm sure we'll find time."

She didn't want to talk to him. She didn't want to hear that he had someone else. She didn't want to know that he ditched her because city life had been so much better. Obviously he'd only come back for the babies. He wasn't even here for her now. He was just going to give her some platitudes, and she'd rather not.

But she wouldn't deprive him of the privilege of being able to apologize. She'd taken that privilege without asking, and her steps felt happier, and her soul sweet, even though her sister was still most likely dying, and even though the responsibilities of raising the twins felt heavy on her shoulders.

"All right, we're going to ask you to gown up, just because they're young. You need to scrub right here at the sink, grab a gown from the shelf, put it on, and then you can come in, and we'll take care of you." The nurse waited until they nodded, and then she pointed to the packets of soap and said, "There's soap in those packets. You open it, pour the liquid over your hands and arms, and then use the brush to brush your hands, particularly your fingernail area, and then up your arms. You don't have to brush yourself bloody, but just try to get germs off. And then dry off, and put your gown on."

"All right," Becky said.

"Got it," Rodney added.

They brushed in silence, figuring out how to open the packets and pour them over their arms, using the brush to scrub their skin.

"She didn't say to rinse? We're supposed to rinse, right?" Becky said.

"I can't imagine we're not," Rodney agreed, so they turned the water on, rinsed their arms, and dried them off. They were soon gowned up, and Rodney used his elbow to push the door open, then held it for her so she could walk through.

The room contained multiple bassinets, and Becky looked around, trying to figure out where the nurse was who had just spoken with them.

"Rodney and Becky?" a new nurse said as she walked over to them.

"Yeah," Rodney said.

"All right. Come on over here. We have your babies in the same bassinet. We found that with twins, they're usually calmer when they sense the other one beside them."

"That's interesting. I wouldn't think babies would be able to tell." Becky kind of spoke to herself, and Rodney nodded, giving her a glance and showing her that he agreed.

"Somehow they can," the nurse said, shrugging her shoulders. She seemed very kind but also rather frazzled and busy, although she didn't hurry them.

"We have Marley with the pink hat, and Kevin with the blue." Becky expected the nurse to apologize for using gender stereotypes, but she didn't. And Becky was glad. They could at least tell the difference between the babies now. Because looking at them, they looked very much the same.

"If you need help picking them up, you can ask. Just make sure you support the head," the nurse said.

Becky nodded, and something started beeping loud and shrilly, and the nurse excused herself. "Just give me a holler if you need me. I need to get that."

She hurried off.

"I feel like we didn't get enough instructions," Becky said, looking uncertainly at the babies. Although, the longer she looked at them, the more they looked perfect to her.

"Yeah. I needed a good bit more to feel comfortable. Probably at least six hours more."

"We can do this. We're responsible adults, and people raise babies all the time." Becky sighed. "Right?"

"Can I be honest?" Rodney asked, and she looked up at him. That was a question he normally wouldn't ask at any point in their friendship. It made her sad that he had to ask it now.

"I expect you to be honest." She met his eyes, and a silent message passed between them. They used to talk like that all the time, but this was the first time that she actually felt the old bond they used to have.

"I think they're ugly. They look like little scrunched-up monkeys, and I don't see anything cute about them. I sure hope they grow out of that stage."

She wanted to laugh. But she looked back at the babies instead. She was a little offended. Maybe if they were her babies, she could have laughed, but they were Rita's babies, and she felt like she needed to defend her sister.

"I guess I can see the monkey resemblance, but their cheeks are so perfect and their little mouths are just adorable." Their eyes were scrunched up, and she couldn't really see the rest of their bodies, because they had them wrapped in towels or maybe a special blanket, but they looked like kitchen towels.

"All right, I can do this," Becky said. She tried to figure out the best way and decided that she was most comfortable with the head in her left arm for some reason. Maybe that was so that her right arm would be there to catch it if she dropped it. That didn't sound like the best reason, but she just kept that information to herself. Surely she wasn't going to drop the baby.

She put her arm underneath the head and awkwardly managed to get baby Marley into the crook of her elbow.

There was a rocking chair right beside the bassinet, and she thought that she would probably have less chance of dropping her if she sat down, so she carefully scooted around the front of the rocking chair and sank into its depths.

Now she wasn't going to move for a very long time. Preferably until the baby was old enough and big enough to crawl on her lap on its own and she wouldn't have to worry about dropping it.

"All right. You made that look easy." Rodney studied the child still sitting in the bassinet. "But I think I'll just leave him there."

"Really? You're going to let his sister get all the attention? That is not acceptable."

She looked up at him, figuring that he needed a little bit of prompting in order to get the nerve up to do what she had just done. Rodney was brave at some things, but she understood that babies were a completely different story.

Rodney pressed his lips together and gave her an annoyed look, like he knew she was right, that he needed to do it, but he didn't want to.

Still, he shifted around, getting an arm under the baby's head and pulling Kevin up toward himself.

"All right. I understand why you sat down. I should have moved another rocking chair over beside you to begin with."

"I'm feeling a little more comfortable. Maybe I can do it." She got her right arm and put it around her left, just to give the baby more stability, and then she leaned forward, standing up. Presto. She didn't drop the baby, and she was standing. She felt like she should get applause or something.

"I'd clap, but my hands are full."

"Thank you. I was wondering where my appreciative audience was. I feel like I deserve a standing ovation."

"I'm standing anyway," Rodney joked.

She grinned at him, and he smiled back, and part of her resented the fact that the past had just left, and he hadn't paid for it at all, but that was what forgiveness was. Her saying she would take the check this time. She had it. She paid for it.

And that's what she'd done. She paid, and then she was supposed to forget about it. Wasn't that what Jesus had done for her? He paid, and then it was finished. No one had to pay again, and he didn't keep rubbing it into her face, making her feel bad that she didn't pay.

It was over. And that's what she had to do. Otherwise, the forgiveness that she granted was worthless.

By that time, she'd gone over by the rocking chair that was on the other side of the bassinet and grabbed a hold of the back of it, carefully holding the baby in her left arm.

She slid the rocking chair around the bassinet and got it in position beside hers.

"Wow. That was pretty impressive," Rodney said.

"I was scared the whole time."

It was true. She had been, although she'd been lecturing herself too. And now, grateful that was over, she went back to her chair, positioned herself in front of it, and then sat down carefully, realizing as she did so that she needed to move the baby a bit so she didn't bump her head on the arm of the chair.

"Watch when you sit down that you don't bump his head. It's easy to do. I almost did that time."

"Thanks for the warning," he said, getting ready to settle down, putting his left hand underneath the baby's head. She realized he was holding Kevin in his right arm.

The way they had the chairs positioned, the babies would be "looking" at each other as they sat there.

She was pretty sure that the babies couldn't recognize each other, since it would have been dark in the womb, and she wasn't sure the babies' brains were developed enough for them to actually see anything and know what it was.

"How old are they before they can look at something and recognize it?" she asked.

"You mean they can't do that right now?" Rodney asked.

"I don't think so." She blew out a frustrated breath. "I'd like to Google it right now. I should have been doing this before. But I didn't realize I was going to want to know all these things. Need to know them."

"Me either. I guess I knew that we were getting babies, but it didn't dawn on me how much information I was going to want to know."

"'You don't know what you don't know,' right?" she said. It was something that they had said to each other over their teenage years as they found out new things that surprised them.

"That's right, Beckpet."

The nickname that he had for her rolled off his tongue almost like it was a habit. Although she knew he hadn't used it for at least five years.

Her back started to bristle at it. She didn't want him to use a nickname. He didn't have permission to be that familiar with her.

But forgiveness.

She forgave. She had to let it go. She couldn't hold on to the resentment and the ill will.

That didn't mean she had to use his nickname.

She kept her eyes on the baby in her arms. Praying for her sister. She just wanted to continuously pray for Rita, that things would go well, that they would get all the cancer, that these babies would know their mom all their lives, that Rita would have a long and healthy life.

"Rodney and Becky?" a low, soft female voice said.

They looked up to see a doctor in scrubs with a hairnet on and the face mask pulled down from in front of her mouth.

"That's us," Rodney said, moving as though he were going to stand up.

"You can stay seated. I just... I just needed to come talk to you. I was with Rita. Is that your sister?" she said, looking at Becky.

Becky nodded.

"All right. She had you two listed on her consent form as the two people we can share her medical information with." The doctor closed her eyes and took a breath.

Then, with compassion flowing out of every pore, she opened her eyes and said, "Dr. Melbourne got the babies, and then I took over. We were hoping to remove the cancerous tumor that had wrapped around her intestines. It was intertwined with her liver and pancreas as well. It was much more involved than what we realized. And if you know much about cancer, you know it takes a lot of blood to feed it, and..." She swallowed. "She bled to death on the operating table. I am sorry that I have to give you this news."

Fifteen

Becky gasped but didn't say anything.

The doctor continued. "I know it's probably not much consolation, but from the look of the tumor, we will send it to pathology, but just from my experience with cancer, she was not going to survive that. Whether she was pregnant or not. It's very, very aggressive and well-integrated into her abdominal cavity. She is very blessed she was able to have the babies delivered when she could. I would say another week, maybe two, and she wouldn't have been with us anyway."

Becky couldn't speak. She tried to swallow and process. Not only was her sister gone, dying on the operating table, but the doctor said even if she had survived the operation, she wouldn't have survived long.

"What if she had been treated back when she was four or five months along in the pregnancy? In other words, if she had her pregnancy terminated?"

"Well, obviously, I don't have all the information. Normally I would have scans to look at and to compare and to say, 'well, it grew this much, and when we first found it, here's what it looked like.' But we don't have those comparisons. So I can't say for sure." The doctor waited for them to nod, making sure they understood.

"But in my opinion, my professional opinion, seeing these things every day, I would say yes. She might have had a good chance of surviving the cancer if she had chosen to terminate pregnancy and been treated immediately. I can't say for sure. Again, I don't know how this cancer would respond to chemo, until we test and see what kind of cancer it is. But with the combination of chemo and radiation to shrink it and surgery to possibly remove the tumor. Yeah. She might have survived."

She took a breath, and then she tilted her head over. "I probably ought to say that it's just as possible that she wouldn't have. With a tumor this big, this aggressive, this integrated into her abdominal cavity, it's quite possible that there are other places I didn't see, because I didn't go looking around for more. It's possible that she wouldn't have made it anyway. So, she made a decision. Obviously it didn't turn out well for her, but we do have two live babies, and had she terminated the pregnancy, we could have ended up with three dead humans."

The doctor's lips flattened, and she didn't look happy about either outcome, but she waited, standing in front of them, almost as though she were preparing herself for an onslaught.

Becky supposed there were people who attacked the messenger. Who accused her of incompetence, of not doing her job, and were angry that she couldn't save everyone. Becky wasn't going to do that.

"Thank you for your effort. I know that she was a complicated case, and I appreciate you taking her on, even though the outcome wasn't what anyone wanted." Obviously. No one wanted a dead body especially if the dead body belonged to one's sister. Her beautiful, laughing, happy sister. The sister that had asked her for one last thing.

That was to get along with Rodney so that they could raise her babies in a stable, loving home. The stable, loving home she and her sister hadn't had.

How could she say no?

Still, even though she'd forgiven Rodney, she didn't want to live with him. She didn't want to spend any more time with him than what she had to, because she could tell she was still susceptible to him. He could have her under his spell again in no time at all, and he obviously didn't really care about her. When he'd gotten out in the world and seen what other women were out there, he realized how Becky really didn't measure up.

It was something she suspected all along. That she didn't measure up to other people, other women who were raised in normal homes with good families, who didn't sneak into boys' rooms looking for food in the middle of the night when they were ten years old, and who hadn't run away from their foster home so that they could see their sister.

"I'm sorry," the doctor said, pulling her lips between her teeth. "I wish the outcome could have been different."

"I do too. But I appreciate your competence and your willingness, and I'm sorry that you had to tell us such bad news." Becky didn't know what else to say. She wanted to go somewhere and cry, but she was holding the baby, and sitting in the middle of the room, and... Maybe it just hadn't sunk in yet. Her sister wasn't coming back. Maybe she needed to see a body in order to understand.

"There will be people getting in touch with you so that you can discuss things with them and make arrangements. Someone will come find you. So don't worry about looking for anyone. You stay here and love on your babies."

The doctor turned around and walked out of the room, her walk brisk and businesslike, and Becky wondered what else her day held. Were there more surgeries? Did this shake her confidence? Did this make her question her decision to become a doctor and a surgeon in the first place? Did she wonder why she fought a disease that always seemed to win? Or did it not bother her at all? Was this just a job, just one more person who didn't make it. And then she was going to move on to the next person with the goal of curing them but detached emotionally from the end result?

Becky didn't think she could have a job like that without somehow emotionally detaching herself. She couldn't stand to deliver the sad news to hopeful family members, couldn't stand to see the blood on the operating table and know that her skills were too little and too late.

"That job would suck." Rodney somehow managed to encapsulate what she was feeling and thinking into four words.

"Really?"

"You think she has more surgeries today?" he asked.

"I don't know. I was just thinking that I would have to become emotionally detached in order to do that job."

"Yeah. How do you lose a patient and then move on to the next one. Without...doubting yourself. Or wondering if you were in the right profession."

"Yeah. Or wanting to quit your job and go be a burger flipper at McDonald's. No stress, if you burn the burger, just pitch it, and stick another one on the grill."

"Right? It's not a matter of you just upended someone's life, now you're going to see what you can do in some other family."

"Yeah. I guess... Guess I wouldn't want a job with that kind of stress and strife, but I'm glad that there are people who do that, because... Well, first of all, because we have Kevin and Marley. But also because, until the very end, we had hope. If there hadn't been someone to do the surgery, we wouldn't have hope at all. She gave us hope, and she gave Rita hope."

"Do you think? I got the distinct feeling that Rita knew she wasn't going to make it."

Again, Rodney said exactly what she had been thinking.

"Yeah. I got the feeling too." She didn't know what to make of it though. "I guess I just don't understand how she could have known. Maybe she had a premonition, or maybe it was negative thinking, and it came true."

"There is something to that. What's the quote? 'If you think you can or you can't, you're right.'"

"Yeah. I guess thoughts do matter. I think they matter more than we think they do, but we just aren't cognizant enough to realize that actions follow our thinking."

"I've often wondered why the Bible tells us to focus on thinking the good things, like that verse in Philippians, where it tells us to focus on whatsoever things are pure and right and good and all that."

"Yeah. I definitely think that God knows. After all, He made us. He knows exactly how we work and that what we think impacts what we do."

"I wish He would emphasize that a little more, you know? Like, 'hey, this is serious stuff, brain science, and you need to live by it.'"

"I still don't think people would listen, even if God had said that. But isn't that what the whole Bible is? Brain science? And we just kind of brush it off as old-fashioned and out of date. But when you practice the principles, they work."

It was interesting, Becky had just experienced that that morning. She had forgiven, and immediately she had felt lighter, better, like she had been scrubbed clean on the inside. God's principles work. It was just humans who thought they had a better way. None of it sounded good, because it was hard, it was too much, they didn't want to do it. But if they would just knuckle down and get started, it happened.

Becky realized that all of their conversation was avoiding what the most important thing was. Her sister was gone.

She felt her throat tightening and her eyes clogging up with tears.

She hadn't believed it was going to happen. She had wanted to think that she could, by sheer force of will, drag her sister through the cancer fight, fight it for her, and be victorious on the other side.

Obviously, God had other plans, and who was she to question those plans?

"Are you okay?" Rodney asked, leaning over like he could feel her emotions trying to get the best of her.

"I think I'm going to need to go somewhere and cry." Becky didn't want to admit that. She wasn't sure that Rodney had ever seen her cry.

"You probably don't need to go anywhere. I don't think anyone in this room would hold it against you if you cried because your sister just passed away."

"I can't cry here."

"Why not?"

"You're not crying," she said, her eyes narrowing and her words coming out with more force than she intended. Why was he trying to get her to break down in front of everyone? She didn't do that.

"Maybe I'm waiting for you to start."

She snorted. "I bet."

"You're too prideful, Becky. It's okay to show what you think is weakness. Sometimes showing weakness is actually strength."

"Are you done lecturing me?" She wanted to say that he was a jerk, and he didn't have any wisdom that she wanted to hear, and then she realized he was right. With her words, she just confirmed it. "I'm sorry. You're right. It's pride. I don't want people to see me as weak. But I also just don't want people to see me right now. Is it okay to want to be alone?"

"I suppose." He sighed, and then he said, "I guess I don't want you to leave. I...don't like the idea of you crying by yourself, but I also don't like the idea of being alone right now. I... I'm a little bit scared."

There. She looked away. He'd been vulnerable too. He had accused her of pride, and then he'd gone and shown her that maybe what she saw on him was just a veneer as well. A prideful veneer, designed to not allow anyone to see that he was afraid and didn't want to be alone.

Is that what he meant about her not crying by herself?

No. She wasn't going to try to grasp at straws, trying to prove to herself that somehow he cared. She was not going to do that. He had been clear, and she could accept it and be okay with that.

"We've been holding the babies for more than an hour. Let's set them down. We'll tell the nurses that we're leaving, and we'll find somewhere quiet, okay?"

She didn't want to go somewhere with him. She didn't trust him. But she did want to go. As much as she loved holding the baby in her arms and feeling comforted by the feel of it, she needed to get up, needed to move, needed to process somehow, and she knew the movement would help her.

"All right." She looked down at Marley's little face. The baby would never know her real mother. Except, Becky would make sure she knew Rita, knew how beautiful she was. How strong and independent and sweet and kind and all of the good characteristics that made up her sister. Marley would know.

She wiggled to the edge of the rocking chair, feeling like she'd done this before, and each time, it got easier. She held the baby in her arm, pushing up and smiling when she made it to her feet without dropping or hurting her.

Moving to the bassinet, she set Marley down in the same spot where she picked her up.

Rodney had managed to get up too, and he moved over to the other side of the bassinet.

The nurse must have seen the moving, and she came over, smiling a bit. "You two are leaving?"

"Yes. We just found out their mother passed away. We...need to take a walk. But we want to come back." Rodney looked at the nurse, and Becky prayed that she wasn't going to tell them that no other time was open, and they couldn't see the babies again until the next day.

"All right. They'll be here when you get back. If you have trouble finding it, just ask for directions for the visitor entrance to the NICU. You need to scrub up every time you come in."

The nurse smiled, and they nodded.

"We're in the NICU," Becky whispered as they walked out.

"I guess."

"They didn't seem like they had any problems."

"Maybe that's just where they take babies that they're not sure about. I don't know."

"Or maybe they didn't have room anywhere else, and they wanted them to have a good eye on them. But it seems like the nurses are busier with much sicker babies."

"Yeah. I feel bad for those parents, and is it terrible to be grateful that it's not us?"

"Or maybe, we just don't realize that they're looking for something?"

"I suppose it's possible too."

All sorts of terrible things came into Becky's mind. Maybe they had the babies in there for observation because they were afraid the cancer had spread. Maybe they were going to take a look at the babies, except... They would need to get Rodney's and her permission, since Rita wasn't around to give it to them. They'd have to ask before they did anything, right?

She wasn't sure how this new process worked, but it was obvious they were going to need to figure it out. Not for the first time, she was grateful that she had Rodney beside her.

Sixteen

"I feel like the hospital is really taking a chance on us," Rodney said as he opened the door to Rita's apartment and held it while Becky walked in, carrying Kevin in his car seat.

The babies were forty-eight hours old, and the hospital had declared them healthy and had released them.

He knew Becky felt overwhelmed, because she had also had an appointment set up to talk to the funeral director about Rita's arrangements.

Plus, if she was feeling even half as nervous as he was with these babies, she had more than enough to deal with.

"I agree. They should come with an owner's manual or something."

He thought about the Bible, but he knew that wasn't what she was talking about.

"I know that the nurse watched me when I gave her a bath, but I was more concerned about not dropping her and not having the nurse yell at me than I was about figuring it all out, you know?" He wished he would have paid better attention, but he was paying really good attention at the time. Just not to the things that bothered him now.

One of the babies started to fuss, and Becky looked down. "Is it feeding time again already?"

He checked his watch. "I think so. I'm pretty sure we fed them at six or seven this morning, and then by the time the doctors got in and the nurses did all the paperwork and we did all the signing...it's ten. I think they should be hungry."

At least they didn't really have to worry about them starving to death since Marley was going to wake up and start screaming. Kevin was a little bit more laid-back. But he'd demand to be fed too. Marley would eat and then start crying an hour later, and they couldn't figure out whether she had a tummy ache or whether she was hungry or whether she was just frustrated that she couldn't boss the world around yet.

Rodney had a feeling that Marley took after her Aunt Becky, and it was the third option.

He hadn't told Becky that yet. He hadn't said much of anything to Becky. They'd been dealing with all the forms and the signatures and the things that they had to sign and have notarized and made a couple of trips to the notaries and one to the lawyer's office, and the babies were officially theirs, pending paperwork, but they were both absolutely exhausted. Becky even more so, because she was also processing the death of her sister. The hospital had a policy that the babies could be taken care of by the caregivers, so since they didn't have an official room, they had a little room off to the side that the hospital staff called the transition room.

They had given it to Rodney and Becky along with the twins.

It had a double bed, which was not big enough for both of them to sleep on without touching, so only one of them slept at a time.

Rodney had not figured out what he was going to do or where he was going to stay, but he knew he could not stay with Becky.

He'd lived with a woman for three months, and it had ended in heartache and disaster and with him engaging in a sin that he never thought he would be susceptible to, considering how his whole body and soul had been focused on Becky.

But he understood the danger of proximity and knew that living with Becky could not be an option for him. Not unless they were married, and he hadn't apologized, hadn't explained about the possibility that he had a son, and while Becky seemed to have been sincere about forgiving him and didn't seem to hold anything against him, he didn't feel like their relationship was at the point where they were back to being good friends, let alone ready to have any kind of romantic elements in it.

But he was hopeful that they would get there. They just had a lot of things to work out first.

And they had to take care of these babies.

Marley had erupted into the loud, mewing screams that signaled she needed attention and she needed it now.

Kevin was slowly waking up, probably because his sister was screaming. Pretty soon, he would join her. Not so loud, not so demanding, but in his own laid-back way, he'd be letting them know.

"The hospital gave us formula, so I'll go mix up two bottles."

"All right. I'll...set them down, I guess, and start getting them out."

He figured out that a car seat was a really nice place to keep them. That was just in the last few hours while they were doing the hospital paperwork and the kids were strapped in. The car seats could be lifted up, swung around, or even rocked with one's foot while one was using one's hands to sign the never-ending stack of papers the hospital threw at them.

"I guess we never went to the store and got anything..." Becky sighed, and she sounded weary. He wanted to say he would watch the babies while she slept, but he figured there were things she wanted to do, like washing sheets and getting a place ready to sleep. He wasn't sure whether there was more than one bedroom in this apartment, but maybe she wouldn't even be interested in sleeping in her sister's bed.

He had no idea. They hadn't had time to talk, and she hadn't had time to process Rita's death.

For the next forty-five minutes, they focused on feeding the babies, changing them, burping them, and holding them while they went back to sleep.

"I think we're good for another couple of hours," he said softly.

Just then, Kevin fussed a bit, and he thought maybe he had spoken too soon.

Becky shot him a withering glance.

"Sorry," he mouthed, barely allowing a wisp of the sound to leave his lips.

She smiled and rolled her eyes. Saying that she was just kidding. It wasn't his fault that the babies fussed.

Kevin settled back down, and with a last look at the babies back in their car seats on the floor, Becky stood and grabbed her notebook and pen, and then collapsed on the couch.

He was sitting on the recliner, his forearms on his knees, watching her.

"All right. I guess we should take this quiet time to try to figure some things out."

He wanted to point out that if she had met him at the Blueberry Beach diner when she said she was going to, they could have had at least some of it figured out, but he knew that wasn't the slightest bit true. Not only was it not her fault her truck wouldn't start, but while it was less than a week ago, they had had no idea, absolutely none, of what they were getting into. At least he hadn't. This had been a lot different than what he had been expecting.

"Do you have an appointment today? Later?" he asked before she could say anything else. He didn't want her to have to run and do all the shopping and then also run to the appointment. She would be running all day, and...he didn't mind taking care of the babies, but he wanted to make sure that she wasn't doing everything.

Her face clouded, although her words were clear. "Yes. With the funeral director, at two o'clock." She looked down at her paper but did not write anything. It was like she couldn't meet his eyes, couldn't allow herself to feel anything, or she would break into a million little pieces.

He knew she was trying to hold it together because they had responsibilities, but he wished that she felt easy enough in his presence that she could let her guard down just a bit.

But he knew Becky. She hadn't let her guard down at all. Even though they talked about it in the NICU, sitting there, and she understood there was probably a pride thing, she still just was that private of a person. He probably shouldn't needle her about it being pride. Maybe it was, a little bit anyway, but he understood that some people just needed some privacy. That having people around was too much.

"All right. It doesn't seem fair that you have to run out to do the grocery shopping and then also go to meet with the funeral director."

"So you're saying you don't want to be stuck here with the babies all day?" she asked, a little smile turning one corner of her lips up but also concern in her eyes. She really didn't want him to have to do anything that made him uncomfortable.

This whole situation was uncomfortable. She was way too late for the party if she was trying to keep him from feeling uncomfortable. But he understood. She was trying to ease his burden. That was something that came naturally to Becky. Even though she was also naturally bossy.

"No. I'm happy to stay here with the babies all day. I'm a little nervous, but I have your cell phone number, and I'm not afraid to use it."

She gave him a tight smile. "We also need to set up a doctor's appointment in two weeks. They said they were going to do that at the hospital, but they never did."

"I think they were kind of discombobulated because we're not the normal family."

"That's a good point. I agree. They did seem at times to be stymied about what to do with us."

That was probably part of the reason that it took them so long to discharge them. Unless hospitals just were naturally incompetent when it came to paperwork.

"I agree. But we're through that now. I'm happy to watch the kids, if you're happy to do the shopping and the meeting."

"I am. I...might be able to get the funeral director to come here. He had mentioned possibly meeting at the hospital, but I didn't want to meet him there." Her voice trailed off a bit, and he thought he understood. Planning her sister's funeral was going to take more strength than she had at the hospital.

"That's a good idea. You want me to call and see if he will?"

"Yeah. Could you do that while I'm shopping?"

"As long as the babies aren't crying."

"All right. We have that taken care of then," she said, seeming pleased that she could at least check something off her list.

He wanted to talk to her about why he had not talked to her for five years. Why he had turned away from her. She seemed to put it aside, although there was still some kind of barrier between them. And she had enough on her plate. So, he just sat and allowed her to talk about stuff that he figured would work itself out anyway.

"All right. We probably should make a schedule. I assume you have work to do and you need to be gone for most of the day?"

"What about your horses?" Suddenly he realized that she hadn't left the hospital once to drive back to Raspberry Ridge to take care of them at all. "Do you have someone taking care of them indefinitely?"

She opened her mouth and took a breath as though she were going to speak, and then she closed it. And then she looked at the notebook as she said, "Yes. They're taken care of."

That was a weird response. He narrowed his eyes at that.

"You didn't tell me about your business. How much time do you need during the day? Twelve hours?"

"So you would just watch the kids for twelve hours during the day, and then we split the night shift?"

He wasn't sure what she was going to do, and he realized he was avoiding her question. For some reason, he didn't want her to know that he had sold his business. He didn't want her to see the sacrifice. To understand that he had given up everything that was important to him for these babies. Maybe part of that reason was because he hadn't been willing to give it up for her five years ago. Or even before that. He wanted to be successful when he finally came and asked her to marry him. And yet... Wasn't giving it up now partly because he would be with her?

He didn't recall thinking about that when he had decided to sell, but maybe that was in the back of his mind. The idea that he would be with Becky. And he had made enough money for now. He had pushed aside the people who were in his life, and most important to him, in order to focus on something that he realized now wasn't necessary. He had more than enough money with which to live comfortably, why hadn't he been happy? Content?

But she was going to find out sooner or later, and he didn't want her to think he was hiding more things from her. He had enough bombshells to drop on her. Eventually.

"I sold my business. I had someone who I knew would buy if I mentioned I was selling, and I was right. I still have a few different things to hash out, but... I can be here full-time."

Her mouth opened wide, and she blinked.

"What are you going to do to earn a living?" she asked, and her tone held shock and concern.

He smiled and laughed a little at her obvious concern for him.

"I sold my business," he said again, and that time, he emphasized the word "sold." "I have a lot of things I need to tell you, but you have a lot on your plate, and I didn't want to add more to it. But for right now, let me just say that when I sold my business, I got rid of about seventy percent of the work that I have to do, which includes all the work that I need to do in the office. I can unload my office space, and I'm in the process of having my lawyer do just that. But the bottom line is, I'm set for life. I don't have to worry about working, or money, again. I'm not going to be extravagantly wealthy, but I'm talking I have tens of millions in the bank and in various investments."

There. It was far more than he needed to say. He could have just said, *I've got money, don't worry about it.* But he wanted her to understand that it wasn't a matter of having a limited amount of money. While the money that he had was finite, it was also far more than they needed.

"All right. Wow." She looked back down at her notebook and stared at it, either processing what he said or unsure what to write about that. How does one put down, *he has more money than we could ever need*?

"Now tell me about your horses," he said, wanting to know how long the person who was watching them was going to be available. "How soon do you have to go and relieve the person who's doing the work?" He squinted at her. "Do you have bookings that you need to be there for?"

"No. I sold them."

He blinked, then straightened and pulled back, shock radiating through his body. "You sold your horses?"

"You sold your business," she said, looking at him like it wasn't any bigger deal than what he had done.

"But I didn't want my business. I didn't love it. And I just sold a piece of it. A piece that I was brokering that was set to make me a billionaire. I…" He paused and looked around. "I know we're supposed to be talking about the babies and the schedule and the things we're going to do, but…"

"And that's what we need to talk about. I sold my horses, you sold your business, I imagine we probably both did it for the same reason. I wanted to be able to do the best I could for my sister and her babies, and to do that, I needed a reliable vehicle, and I needed to be able to leave without being tied to the stable. I also lived above the stable, and it wasn't a fit place to bring the babies home to. Selling the horses enabled me to buy a reliable vehicle and move down here permanently. Or as long as my sister needed me."

She looked down. Obviously her sister didn't need her at all anymore, other than for her to keep her word about the babies.

"Wow. I'm sorry, you can't hit a guy with that and not give him a chance to breathe."

After hearing what she had done, he knew it was time. He couldn't keep from telling her any longer. He stood, walked over to the couch, and held his hand out. She looked at it.

"What?" she asked, giving him a puzzled look. And then her eyes went back to his hand.

"Take it."

Her lips pressed together, but she put the pen down on the table beside her, put her hand in his, and rose, standing before him in front of the couch.

They stood face-to-face, close enough that he could feel her breath on his neck and feel the heat that radiated from her body. See the pupils of her eyes and the fine lines that were at the corners where they didn't used to be.

"Five years ago, I lost everything. I had been trying to build a fortune, you knew that. Learning business, investing, and trying to… basically trying to become rich. But I wanted to learn to be a businessman. I wanted to be able to support you in the way that you deserved."

"I didn't want that," she said.

"I know. You know how many times over the last five years I

thought back to how the more I seemed to live for money, the more you tried to tell me that you didn't want it and seemed to actually start to hate having money."

She looked away. She knew he was right.

"Anyway. I made a couple of risky decisions, because I was getting impatient. They should have made me money, and fast, but I ended up losing everything. I had to declare bankruptcy, although I paid every penny that I owed back, with interest. Even to people who wouldn't have made me pay them back."

"I wouldn't have expected anything less from you," she said, and there was a tremor in her voice.

"But I was ashamed to face you. I was ashamed for you to know that I wasn't the big businessman that I was trying to be. That I had failed miserably, failed hard, failed spectacularly bad, and I just didn't want you to look at me and see someone who was less than."

"Rodney. I saw you at your worst."

He knew she was talking about his high school years, when he'd stepped off the straight and narrow and become rebellious and dabbled in things he shouldn't have, definitely walking away from the Lord for a while.

"I guess I didn't see it that way. I wanted to build back better, for you to see that I was successful. I wanted to go to you, not as a pauper who had been stupid and lost everything but as a rich man who could offer you the world."

"Yeah, that's nice," she said, sounding unimpressed.

"Everyone I talked to advised me against it. They told me to be honest with you. They told me that you would understand that I made mistakes, that I failed, but you wouldn't understand why I shut you out. But I just didn't listen. It was my pride."

She pressed her lips together, probably remembering their conversation a few days ago, when he'd accused her of being prideful and that was why she didn't cry in front of people. Maybe he was wrong. Maybe she just wanted privacy. But he knew it applied to him.

"So you didn't hate me?" she asked, and it seemed to be a hard question for her.

"Of course not! I loved you. I love you more than life." He couldn't help himself. His hands came up, and he gripped her upper arms, wanting her to look up to him. "That's why I didn't. Because I loved you and I was ashamed. I didn't think that you could look at me and love me the way I was. I felt like I needed to have money and be successful in order for you to see someone who was worthy of you, because that's what I felt like you deserved. A successful, rich, smart man, who deserved the amazing woman that you are."

She pursed her lips and seemed to be fighting herself. "I want to believe you, but...my letters were returned unopened, you changed your number or blocked me or something. I couldn't get a hold of you. Even if I was hurt or dying, I couldn't tell you." Her tortured eyes lifted to his. "I loved you. I loved you, and you abandoned me."

"I know who you are. I knew it then. I knew you'd wait for me." She looked away, and he remembered that there was someone else.

She didn't say anything, even though he waited. Would she tell him?

In the heat of the moment, in his need to tell her, explain to her what he'd done, he'd forgotten. How could he have forgotten something like that?

Of course, after the week he had, it was amazing that he remembered his own name.

"Do you have someone else?" he asked. He didn't want to ask. He wanted her to tell him, but he couldn't stand the suspense. Maybe she did have someone, and she wasn't interested in him. Maybe he had just wasted his time.

But no, he needed her to know. Even if they didn't end up together. He needed to know.

"No. There isn't anyone else. I was with a guy, but I think he saw me as his designated driver. He wasn't you."

That's all she said, but it said everything to him. He knew that this was a hard time, but he couldn't keep himself from smiling hugely.

"Nice," he said softly, his words drawing her eyes to his face.

"You don't need to smile at that." She looked annoyed.

"Why not? I like it that you're not with the guy anymore, because he's not me. Isn't that something for me to smile about?"

"Maybe I'm just not with the guy because no one else thinks I'm worth being with. Even you didn't have a problem dumping me without a word."

She yanked her shoulders away and walked around him, over to the kitchen.

So that was the problem. He'd hurt her, and what he'd done made her think she wasn't good enough. That she wasn't worth anything. He wasn't sure how some other guy hadn't snapped her up, but it wasn't because she wasn't worth it. She was certainly more than worth it. She was worth everything.

"I think you might be surprised at the men who would like to have you but are maybe a little bit afraid of you. I probably would be too if I hadn't grown up with you."

"So now I'm scary," she said, going around the counter like she needed to have something between them. It was a small space, but maybe she felt more protected now that they were separated.

He walked over until he was over on the other side of the counter, and he leaned on it.

"Becky. I think you know you're scary at times. I also think you know I love that about you. I love that you're fierce, unafraid, that you fight with passion and integrity and stubbornness and all the determination in your huge heart, for the people you love. Like your sister. You sold your horses for your sister." That was why she did it. She loved her sister, and she had a huge, fierce heart that wouldn't allow her to do anything less. Sure, she loved her horses, but she understood they were just things. Becky wasn't the one who got confused about that. That was him.

Seventeen

Becky forced herself not to retreat anymore, like there was any place for her to go. She had moved back, putting the kitchen counter between them, because... It was too hard for her to stand there face-to-face. She felt too vulnerable.

Then he called her scary and made her feel like there was something wrong with her.

She knew he didn't really mean it, but still, the idea that she was fierce wasn't exactly a compliment when he said it like that.

"I think we should focus on what we need to do right now. You're right. I'm overwhelmed with everything else, and I don't really want to talk about this right now." There. She said it. Five years ago, she would have loved to talk to him. She wanted to hash it all out, but now... Now it just hurt and felt terrible, and she didn't know whether to believe him or not. After all, it made sense, but if he loved her, would he really have shut her out?

Maybe she just needed to process it.

"As you wish," he said, pushing back away from the counter and going back over to the living room, checking on the babies.

"It seems like once they're asleep, it doesn't matter how much we talk, they don't wake up," he said, very casually, like he hadn't just been baring his heart to her.

Maybe he wasn't. Maybe he was just feeding her a line.

She knew Rodney wasn't like that. Not the Rodney that she used to know. But she really didn't know this man. He'd only been back for less than a week, after five years of absolute silence.

"All right. I think I have figured out what we need. I can go right now and get the stuff. I'm just going to get necessities. They sent us home with a lot of diapers, but we definitely need bottles and something to clean them with."

"Okay."

She listed a few more things off. He agreed, but then he said, "Are we gonna stay here?"

She looked up at him. Her eyes wide. She didn't have anywhere else to stay.

"I'll have to go through Rita's things. She didn't go over anything with me. But the rental info is in there somewhere, I'm sure. I... I don't know if she was current or not."

"How would you feel about buying a place in Raspberry Ridge?"

"Um... For you?"

"For you and the babies. I... I wouldn't stay there."

She stared at him. He was offering to buy a house for her and the babies. Or just a place for them to stay.

"What would be the agreement? I can stay as long as I'm taking care of the babies?"

"It would be your house. You would stay there with the babies. I would help as much as I can, be there all day, but... I don't think it's a good idea for me to live there."

"No. It's not a good idea for us to live together. I agree completely. I guess I just figured until we figure this out, we were probably going to have to spend some nights together, but we wouldn't be sleeping or anything."

"Right." He closed his lips and didn't look super happy, but he didn't say anything else.

"So you have a problem with that?" she asked. That was what they were supposed to be doing—talking about stuff, not getting angry, pushing their lips together, and looking away.

"No. I don't. You're right. And I guess I was just thinking I wasn't sure whether you would get upset if I told you that I already had a real estate agent on it, and they found a house with stables and forty acres just a little north of Raspberry Ridge. It's not right on the lake, and there are no lake views, but it's within walking distance of town. So, we could walk down our lane and walk into town. But if you're looking for something with a lake view—"

"I was living in an unfinished one-room apartment above the stable. I'm not picky about whether or not I get a lake view." She didn't really want to admit where she'd been, but the idea that she would be picky about whether or not she had a lake view was absolutely ridiculous. "But we don't need a stable. We don't need forty acres. I... I cannot allow you to buy me a house. But I will however allow you to provide a place for the babies and me to stay...for I don't know how long. I guess I need a little bit of time to figure things out."

She'd already talked to Vera about how she probably wouldn't be able to clean her house for a bit, but hopefully they could work things out. It felt like she'd been trying to do that for a while, and every time she got close, they started talking about something that didn't matter. Or something that mattered too much and she couldn't focus on the day-to-day living.

"All right then. I would really like for you to look at it, but I've been assured that it's in pristine condition and move-in ready."

"I'm not sure where you're talking about, but it might be the house that was just built. People came in, built it, and I think the husband's company transferred him to Oklahoma or something. And they had to put it up for sale." She didn't always get the gossip around town, but there had been some chatter about that. She'd been especially interested in it because the woman had seemed to be a horse lover. But she had Arabians, and Becky had not really been interested in them. Although she loved watching them. They were beautiful horses.

"It sounds like it might be the same place. My realtor said something about that."

"All right."

She supposed she needed to stop worrying about the future and just take it day by day. So he was going to buy a place. She was allowed to stay there. That was the best she could do for right now.

"If I hurry, I might be able to get back before the babies wake up. Are you okay if I go?"

He nodded, not looking particularly pleased, but she thought that was more because he felt like they still had things to talk about and they didn't have everything hashed out that he wanted to.

She knew the feeling, and maybe she was running away, just a little.

She grabbed her coat, her purse, and her keys and hurried out the door.

The one nice thing about Rita's place in the suburbs of Chicago was that it wasn't far to the nearest store, and she was able to get everything in less than half an hour.

She really wanted to buy a whole pile of baby equipment, but her car wouldn't be able to hold everything she needed plus what she wanted. Not to mention, Rita's apartment was too small anyway. For now, the babies could sleep in their car seats. But they were going to need cribs or bassinets or something.

She also made a quick stop to grab some lunch and pick up a few groceries. In all, she was gone for forty-five minutes. That was unheard of in Raspberry Ridge. It took almost that long to just get to a grocery store.

Still, she would rather have the drive than live in the city. Although, she wasn't going to complain about convenience.

When she unlocked the door to Rita's apartment, Rodney was standing on the other side.

She didn't hear any crying, so she assumed the babies were still asleep.

He pulled the door open and held it while she walked in.

"Everything good?" she asked in a soft voice as she carried the bags to the counter. She figured he was right. Once the babies were asleep, it didn't seem to matter how loud they were, but maybe new noises after silence would bother them. Regardless, it seemed prudent to talk softly.

"Everything's fine. I take it you have more stuff in the car?"

"I do. I can walk out with you. I think if we each make a trip, we'll bring it all in."

"I didn't know if you got any baby paraphernalia that might be pretty big?"

"No. I thought about it, but first of all, Rita's apartment isn't that big, and second of all, if we're moving... I just didn't know." It hurt to think about moving away from Rita. Like leaving her apartment meant she was really gone. She had to push those thoughts away, or she wasn't going to be able to function.

"I talked to my real estate agent while you were gone, and if we want to drive up and take a look at it, we can. I know you have...a funeral to plan, and I can help you with that too. So it's totally up to you."

Her heart squeezed. "Did you call the funeral director? Could he meet us here?"

"Yeah. He's coming at two o'clock," he said as they reached the car and she clicked the key fob so that the back opened.

She wasn't used to this whole key fob thing, but the used-car salesman had given her a quick rundown before she'd driven it out of the lot.

There wasn't much storage space, but she'd been able to get everything in.

"This looks like a lot of stuff for two little kids."

"I bought lunch, and I bought a few groceries so we had something to eat tonight and tomorrow. I... I seem to be incapable of planning long-term, because it's just not settled in my mind what's going to happen."

"All right. Well, maybe we can get you settled faster. I'll call the real estate agent and tell him we'll meet him at the house at five o'clock this evening. That should give us plenty of time to take care of the babies after the funeral director leaves. I don't think we'll be able to settle on the house superfast, but considering that it's a new construction, maybe I'm wrong."

"Yeah. I knew nothing about it."

Sometimes people were able to pull strings and make things happen quickly, and Rodney seemed like he was that kind of guy, but he didn't used to be, and it was odd to think of him that way. So she didn't say anything.

Eighteen

A t five till two, there was a knock on the door. Rodney had Kevin in one arm and a bottle in the other hand.

Becky sat on the couch with Marley.

"I can get it," he said, scooting to the edge of the recliner. She had already started to get up, but she stopped at his words.

She looked scared. He could count on one hand the number of times he'd seen Becky scared.

He wanted to go over and hold her. But she hadn't seemed very receptive to his explanation of why he hadn't talked to her for the last five years. In hindsight, it was really lame. It sounded terrible as he tried to explain it to her. It was too bad he couldn't figure out five years ago that it was going to be embarrassing and ridiculous to try to explain that he wanted to look like a big shot in her eyes, so he didn't tell her that he lost everything and didn't talk to her for five years.

Of course, at the time, he hadn't known it was going to take so much time to build back. Actually, he had wondered if he would ever be able to build back. He certainly hadn't planned to not talk to her for five whole years. It just turned into that as he kept doing better and better financially. He wanted to be huge by the time he got back and confessed what he had done.

It kind of made sense in his mind still, but it still didn't make sense when it tried to come out of his mouth.

And Becky wasn't impressed. He didn't need to be a rocket scientist to figure that out.

"Hello," he said as he opened the door to a dude who was dressed in a suit, with no tie, the top button unbuttoned, but he still looked very professional with his hair slicked down and an iPad notebook type thing held in his hand, along with some brochures.

"Hi. I'm Mr. Carson, from Carson's Funeral Home. I have a two o'clock appointment with Mrs. Becky Rivers?"

"Yeah. You're at the right place. I'm her...friend."

Not boyfriend, not fiancé, not husband. He would rather have said any of those words, but even friend felt like an exaggeration.

As he closed the door and glanced over at Becky, he almost thought she wanted to roll her eyes. She just had a look on her face that said that they weren't friends.

He looked away. He wanted them to be. He wanted them to be more. But even if they were more, underneath that more needed to be a solid foundation of friendship, which meant trust, which meant that when something terrible happened to him, he should trust her and be able to tell her. It also meant that he wouldn't go and sleep with some woman he didn't even like, and barely knew, when he was supposed to be waiting for the only woman who had ever caught his eye and his interest.

Yeah. He hadn't been a very good friend.

"Hello, Mr. Carson. Is it okay if I don't get up?" Becky said as she sat, looking decidedly uncomfortable, on the couch.

"Certainly. I understand."

"You can sit in the chair or here on the couch if you'd like," she said.

"I'll go ahead and sit on the couch," Mr. Carson said, arranging himself and his papers as he sat.

Rodney wondered if he should offer him some refreshments. He decided not to but took his place on the recliner, sitting on the edge, because he didn't feel completely comfortable sitting back. He felt like he needed to protect Becky. But there really wasn't anything for him to do. There was no way to protect her from this. She just had to face it.

He wished that Mr. Carson had taken the recliner so he could at least be beside Becky, close enough to touch her if he needed to.

Maybe he should have stood behind her with a hand on her shoulder.

Something told him she wouldn't have appreciated that right now with their relationship the way it was.

He sat and listened while Mr. Carson talked and then showed Becky the various choices she had.

Becky didn't want to have a huge funeral, and she'd already talked to Rodney about that. It wasn't that she didn't love her sister, it was just there wasn't much extended family, and neither Rita nor Becky wanted to make a big show. She didn't know where to have it or how.

She didn't know what to do, and he could see she was struggling. There were the babies to consider, and it was cold.

"I understand you don't want cremation, but you do know that it's cheaper."

Becky nodded, and she worried her bottom lip.

Rodney thought it might be time for him to step in. "I'm taking care of the expenses for everything, and it doesn't matter what the cost is. Whatever Becky decides, I will be paying for it. In full, and today, if possible."

Mr. Carson raised his brows, and from that point on, he didn't ignore Rodney the way he had when he first came in.

Rodney didn't necessarily need the extra attention, and he hadn't spoken up because of that. He'd spoken up because of the worry in Becky's brows. She sold her horses, and he knew that she might have done it just for the time factor. But she also said about needing to buy a reliable car. He and Rita had talked about that, and Rita hadn't been too concerned about Becky's financial situation, but then Becky had said something about living in an unfinished apartment above the horse stable, and he wondered... How exactly was she making money? It didn't sound like she had any bookings at all, and... Maybe she was worse off than what he thought.

He wondered if he could dig into it without asking her. But he didn't know who he could ask. He had already checked in with Davis and Matt, and they said they hadn't been in touch with her much.

Who else could he check with who wouldn't go straight to Becky and ask?

He always thought that if he wanted to know something, especially about someone he liked and cared about, he should ask them directly. So rather than trying to figure out how he could go behind her back, he decided he would ask her as soon as the funeral director left.

It took an hour to go through all the things, and by then, the babies were done being fed, they had been burped, and Kevin had gone back to sleep. Marley was fussing, and Becky had stood up and was swaying gently back and forth.

"I can take her," he offered as he put Kevin down in the car seat. Kevin stirred a bit but then curled himself back up and settled right back down.

"Thank you," she said. The funeral director had her fill out a couple of forms, and then he said, "I can give you the total now, and if your friend would like to write out a check, that's perfectly fine. Or we can bill you later."

How awkward it must be to have to talk about death and payment all in the same business transaction.

Rodney was glad he had never gone into the funeral business. Although, he had heard that it was quite lucrative.

Becky held her arms out for Marley, and they switched her back. He was close enough to Becky to smell her scent and feel her warmth.

That was how close he wanted to be all the time. He wanted to have the right to stand there.

But he slid the baby back into her arms and prevented himself from lingering. Going to his briefcase, he got his checkbook out and wrote out a check. He hadn't even thought to ask if the man took electronic payments. He almost bet he did. Everybody did nowadays.

Still, it was taken care of now. The mechanics of it anyway. The emotions would linger for a while. He read somewhere that someone who was successful gave himself a limited amount of time to feel bad, and then they forced themselves to look on the positive side and see whatever opportunities had been exposed by the bad thing that happened. It was a ridiculously short amount of time, like thirty minutes or something.

Would he be able to spend thirty minutes being sad about the turns his life had taken and then focus on the positive?

He knew that was a great business asset, to be able to pivot so quickly, and doing it within a matter of minutes would make one almost indestructible. But he doubted Becky would want to let go of her grief so quickly. Although, it would probably make Rita happy to see it happen.

"All right. We'll see you in Raspberry Ridge at the church in two days," the man said, shaking his hand and nodding at Becky, who held the baby, before he left.

Rodney walked over and locked the door after the man walked out.

He turned back around and saw that Becky had turned her back to him and was holding the baby with both arms, hunched over her, as though...was she crying?

"Becky?" he asked, walking softly across the carpeted floor and putting a hand on her back.

She straightened but didn't move away from his touch, which he appreciated. Maybe she didn't hate him, or maybe she just needed another human to share her grief right now.

"That was not what I ever thought I was going to be doing at this stage in my life," she said softly.

"I don't think anybody expects that. Not with her sister. Not at this age."

"I just... I miss her. I see her shoes by the door. Her coat on the hook, her dishes in the cupboard. This whole apartment just is filled with her presence, and I'm holding her babies. But their mom is gone."

"No. I know that's hard." He moved his hand from the middle of her back to her shoulder and pulled her close to him.

She turned, the baby between them.

He slipped down, putting his arm underneath hers and taking the baby from her. He was able to pull her close to him, against his chest, while holding the baby in his other arm.

He felt her arms wrap around him and her back shake silently with tears.

Becky, his fierce, loyal warrior, was crying.

That didn't happen often, and he wished he had both hands around her.

Deciding that it wouldn't hurt, even though the hospital staff had warned against it, he leaned over and carefully laid Marley on the couch.

She stretched without opening her eyes and then curled back up, continuing to sleep.

"Come here," he said to Becky, folding her in his arms and tucking her head under his, and just letting her lean against him and cry. He figured that's probably what she needed. That, or at least to know that someone cared, that someone was there for her, and that she wasn't doing this by herself.

He was imperfect. Very, very imperfect. He had made a lot of mistakes, and he was sure in the future he would make a lot more. But he would be here for her. However she needed him, if she let him.

She cried for a while, and he let her. Even when she stopped, he didn't move and just stroked her hair down her back, and laid his cheek on her head, and was content to just stand there. However long she needed to.

"Sorry," she finally sniffled.

"Don't be. I'm glad. Not that you're crying, but that I could be here. You...need someone. This is an awful lot for one person to carry alone."

"You lost her too. You have babies too. You're taking this too. Why aren't you crying?" She seemed to be angry now, which was how Becky sometimes handled things when she was younger. She'd outgrown that issue as she'd grown older, but he supposed with this trauma before her, she had reverted back to what she knew best.

"She wasn't my sister. I loved her, but not like you did. Remember the whole reason that you and I met was because you couldn't stand to be separated from her, and you ran away from your foster home, which wasn't a very good home, and were living basically in the wide-open area around Raspberry Ridge, trying to feed yourself, so that you could see your sister once in a while." He thought again of how fierce Becky was. How loyal. How deeply she loved. "No wonder it feels like your heart is being broken. She was...part of your heart."

"Yeah. That's right. That's exactly how it feels. That part of my heart is missing."

"And Rita loved you just as much. I was sure of it. Her concern that last night when we were eating was all about you and her babies."

"I don't know if I can raise them. This is all so new. I am surprised I haven't dropped one yet."

"Every parent feels like that the first few weeks. Everything is new. Then, you have another one, and it's all old hat. Then you have a third one, and you wonder what you thought was so hard about it. Except sleep. I don't think you ever get used to not getting any sleep."

She laughed a little, as he had intended, and he moved his face and kissed the top of her head.

She froze. He could feel her body under his arms, just still, like her breath caught in her throat and her heart stopped beating. Then, she pushed away. Not hard, not meanly, but like she'd realized what was going on and needed to keep that protective wall up.

"I'm sorry about that. Thanks for letting me cry. I guess I don't know for sure that I actually needed it or not, but... I appreciate it." She kept her eyes cast down. And then she turned to the couch. "Do you think we can pick her up and put her in her car seat? Or do you think she's okay there?"

"I think she's okay there, but we could put her in her car seat if you need to take a nap. We have a couple of hours until we need to leave to meet the realtor at Raspberry Ridge."

"All right. I wanted to get some laundry done, so maybe I'll do that while I'm waiting."

"Becky," he said, and she stopped in the process of turning away. "Please. Rest."

"I can't. If I lie down, I'm just gonna lie there and think about stuff, and I don't want to do that."

"Please," he said. Knowing that she was exhausted, she had so much that had happened to her, and she just needed to get some rest. "You'll feel better if you're able to sleep for a little bit."

"I know you're right. I know I would feel better, but I'm not tired enough to sleep. I'll just lie there, and things are going to go through my head, and I'm going to feel worse and worse, and I'm going to feel more tired when I get up than I did when I lay down."

"I wish you would try."

"I know how it's going to go. And I'll feel better if I'm busy. I'll at least be able to keep the thoughts at bay."

"Then let me help you."

She laughed. "I promise you, I'm quite capable of putting a load of laundry in the washer by myself. You're right, I'm tired, and I know you're right that I would feel better if I would rest, but I just know that I'm not going to be able to right now."

He let it go. She knew herself better than he did, but he also knew that a person could face things better if they were able to make themselves sleep for a little bit. And that's what Becky needed now more than anything.

He moved around, knowing he had some work that he could probably do while the babies were sleeping, and there were other things to take care of. He supposed that he just needed to let Becky go. Do what she wanted to do. And realize that his right to ask her to do anything was severely limited. She had been kind to him, but she really didn't need to be. And she didn't even know the half of it. How was she going to react when she found out the rest?

Nineteen

"We love the property and would like to make an offer on it," Rodney said as he carried a car seat in each hand, setting them down in the kitchen where the real estate agent stopped, and Becky leaned against the counter. They'd looked at the whole property, leaving the babies in the car with it running while they walked to check the barn and the two outbuildings. One had been billed as a chicken coop and the other as a storage shed.

The house was pristine and looked like it hadn't been lived in at all. It was exactly what they wanted.

"All right. That sounds good."

"There won't be any banks involved," he said, since he was paying cash. "My lawyer said that he would need a couple of days to do some research, and then we can close. Do you think the owners would be willing to do such a quick sale? Especially if we offered ten thousand over the asking price?"

The real estate agent bumbled around a little bit. Rodney got the idea he wasn't used to having someone talk to him like that.

"I can certainly check with them, but I would be willing to bet that they would be ecstatic."

"All right. That sounds good. You'll hear from someone later tonight about sending an offer over."

"That's wonderful. I will keep an eye out for that," the real estate agent said, looking absolutely thrilled.

They shook hands after Rodney put a car seat down. The agent made some small talk as Rodney checked to make sure that the babies were covered with their car seat covers, and then he glanced at Becky, who nodded.

They walked out in the cold while the real estate agent locked the door behind them and made sure all the lights were out, promising to be available for any other questions they might think of on the way home.

Rodney sat one baby on one side, and Becky worked on buckling it in while he went around to the other side and latched that baby in the base of the car seat.

The baby carriers were a real pain in the butt, but he understood about safety and all that. Still, he thought that they could have made it a little less of a hassle to get a kid in and out of the car.

Finally, they were strapped in and ready and headed back to Rita's apartment.

"I'm sorry. I should have thought about what a long drive this was and how hard it would be on you and the babies," he said as he glanced over and saw Becky looking exhausted.

"No. I'm glad that we went and looked at it. I... It was really expensive though, and I'm a little bit concerned," she said, pausing before the word "concern." Like she didn't know what word to use.

"Concerned? What do you mean?" He really didn't understand.

"I don't know. I just feel weird. You're buying a house."

"Beckpet. It's me, Rodney. Your bud. Remember? We used to be really, really good friends. We used to think about being more." He held up a hand. "I'm not trying to insinuate that we should be or anything like that. It's nothing immoral. It's just... Why are you treating me like I'm some stranger being nice to you?"

She gave him a sour look and then turned and looked out the windshield.

Thankfully there were no new snowstorms, and they were getting toward the end of February, which did not necessarily mean spring, but at least it meant that the temperature should hopefully moderate some. Sometimes they got their heaviest snows in March though.

"Because basically you are some stranger being nice to me. It's true that we were friends way back when, but that was a long time ago. We haven't talked in years. We're not that close. In fact, I would say I don't know you any better than I know...most people."

"What would you like to know about me?" he said, trying to keep the hurt out of his voice. He wanted to draw on their years of being close. Their years of doing everything together. How they'd written letters, love letters, to each other. Just because he had made one bad decision, well, two, and five years of silence, did it negate everything that had gone before?

But he supposed it did. It showed her that he wasn't the man that she thought he was. That she couldn't depend on him to stand beside her.

He felt like there was a big, gaping hole in his heart. It was just pouring out pain, and there wasn't anything he could do to stop it. A hole of his own making, and he once again wished he had been a little smarter five years ago.

"Do you really have enough money to afford that house?" she said quietly.

Really? This was about money?

"Yes. I could buy a hundred houses, easily, and still have enough money to live a life of luxury for the rest of my life. I promise you. It's not about the money."

"You said the reason you stopped talking to me was because you lost everything. Could you lose everything again?"

"I got smarter. I lost everything because I got impatient and made some bad decisions. I also didn't diversify like I should have, and as I have now. I also just sold a huge investment that I made, and I made a good bit of money on what I sold. Now, Ford Hansen, who bought it from me, is going to make a lot more, but... That was about seventy percent of what I had. I still have thirty percent of the moneymaking things that take my time and effort, but they're mostly investments. And I'm basically living off the money that my investments are making. I am in the process of investing the money I made from selling, and then I'll have even more than I can live on. I'll just keep that money in investments, live off what I make from it, and everything should be fine. Now, if I wanted to buy a hundred houses like the one we just looked at, I would have to sell or liquidate some of my investments. Does that make sense?"

She had asked, and he wanted to give her the best answer he could.

If she asked if he ever slept with anyone else, he would answer that question too. But he waited, holding his breath and hoping that the things that she wanted to know were not things like that.

"Why? Why are you doing this?"

"Because I promised your sister." That was an easy answer.

"Why did you promise her?"

"Because she asked me. I loved her. Not like you. You are different. You've always been different. But because I loved you, I loved your sister too. I cared about her. And I would have done anything she asked me to do. Just like I would do anything you ask me to do."

That was being raw and real.

They were on the interstate now, and headlights came and went, taillights as well. He kept the speed steady, just under the speed limit. He had precious cargo, and he wanted to be careful. Plus, he didn't want Becky to worry about one more thing, and his driving was one thing he could control.

"What are you going to do?"

"What do you mean what am I going to do?" he asked, confused. Was she talking short-term or long-term?

"With your life. With the babies. Are you planning on being a stay-at-home dad for the next eighteen years? And how are we going to manage this? I know I've already told myself I just need to take a day at a time. Just one minute at a time if necessary, but the future just looks like some big black nothing that I don't understand and don't know how to navigate, and... I can't help but want to at least have some hint of what it's going to look like, you know?"

He wanted to marry her. It had been obvious since the first moment, yes, even in that confrontation at the barn, that he was still madly, wildly, passionately in love with her. All of that, plus there was a calm, strong friend bond that undergirded everything, and he wanted her to feel that too. He wanted that to be part of everything they did.

But she wasn't ready to hear that. And maybe she never would be. He had a few things he needed to say before that could happen. Things that might ruin everything.

"I guess to me the future looks like, yeah. I'll be a work-from-home dad. I'm working on getting rid of my office leases. And allowing my employees time to find other employment before I terminate them. I'm keeping a secretary, a virtual assistant, and my lawyer on retainer. I have an investment banker I work with on commission and just a couple of other people. I'm really paring down. I plan to be home, I plan to have a laptop that keeps me connected, but I'm not going to be jetting all over the place, I'm not going to be going to meetings or highbrowing it with anyone. I've done that, and it's empty. It's empty...without you."

Maybe he shouldn't have said that. He tried to continue quickly and hope that maybe she'd miss it. "So that's what the future looks like to me. I don't know what our living arrangements will be. We already agreed that we can't live together if we're not married. I suppose in my heart of hearts, that's what I want. But I understand that you can't trust me after I ghosted you for five years. So it will take some time, if ever, to get that back. But I wrote you letters, I told you I loved you, and I meant it. I always did. I can't imagine this life with anyone but you. And if you don't feel that way, that's fine. I guess it will be really hard for me to handle seeing you with someone else. But I'll cross that bridge when I come to it. For right now, I'm going to hope and pray that that doesn't happen."

Yeah. He was running at the mouth. Maybe he was more tired than he thought. He kept nagging her to take a rest. Maybe he should follow his own advice. Because he just said way too much.

"I guess you're right. I guess it will take some time. I... I keep thinking you're going to leave me again. I mean it was so sudden. And I was absolutely dumbfounded. And I don't mean to keep rubbing it in. I understand, you were embarrassed and ashamed and all that. Whatever. I get it, I guess. But you've got to see it from my perspective, that I thought you were all in with me, and then you suddenly disappeared.

And it made me feel like I wasn't worth your time or effort. Not even to say goodbye to."

"I am so sorry. I can't change that. I wish I could."

"I know. We can't go back. And I don't mean to rehash the past. I told you I forgive you, and I do. But I suppose while forgiveness carries a lot of I'll bear the cost of that, I'll pay for it, it also doesn't come with an automatic, I'll let you do that again, you know?"

He understood what she was saying. She forgave him, but she couldn't be sure that he wouldn't do it again, and she wanted to put some guards in place so that she wasn't hurt. It would make sense that if he had stolen from her or spit in her face, she might forgive him, but she was going to lock up her valuables and keep a safe distance between them in order to keep those things from happening again.

"I understand. So I guess that kind of defines the future for me. Right now, I've got to take care of the babies, that's number one. Because they can't take care of themselves. But linked very closely with that is number two, and that's trying to prove to you that I'm not going to do that again. Ever." There were a few things they were going to have to hash out, but he skipped over that. Right now, he was trying to establish a friendship again. "I suppose that's what the house is about. We need a place to keep the kids, since being in your sister's apartment is hard for you. Seeing her shoes, her coat, all the things that have her touch on them."

"We're going to have to clean it out eventually," she said softly, looking out the passenger window at the darkness as it flew past.

"I know. But we don't have to do it now. We'll find out where her rent info is at, we'll pay it for a year, and then we don't have to go back if we don't want to."

"I guess I would rather get it done, but... It would be nice to have a month or two to settle into some kind of routine with the babies, and I don't know. Just give some time to pass to get used to the fact that she's not around anymore."

"Again, yeah. I think whenever we do it, it's going to be hard. That's not the kind of thing that's ever going to be easy. But if you give yourself a little bit of time to adjust to this, get caught back up in your sleep, and deal with what's already happened. It probably won't be quite as difficult."

"Thank you. I really do appreciate the time. I was kind of dreading that, along with everything else."

"Don't worry about it. We can take as long as you need to. Even if it's ten years."

She looked across the space that separated them and gave him a little smile. It was encouraging. He wanted more of those. He wanted her to not worry. To not fret. To be perfectly okay with whatever happened.

They were quiet for a bit, and then he broke the silence.

"Is there anything else you want to know about me?" It was a dangerous question, he knew. Because she could ask the one thing that had the potential to blow everything apart. But he was willing to take a chance, because he wanted to be an open book for her. And he was going to tell her anyway, very, very soon. Just wanted to be closer to her first. To make it harder for her to push him away.

"So what have you been doing for the last five years?"

"Specifics? Or in general?" he asked, hoping she was talking about the business.

"You told me you lost everything. Start from there."

"Well, I did. I lost everything. I owed people money, and I didn't have anything coming in with which to pay them. I lost my apartment because I couldn't pay, and I had penalties there as well."

"You had no place to live?"

"Yeah. A friend took me in for a couple of months, but I finally found a cheap, ratty apartment in the absolute worst area of Chicago you can imagine. It was not safe, and it was not good, but it was the right price. From there, I talked to Ford. He was the one who had been advising me all along. He could have bailed me out. And I know on one level, I wanted him to. I was ashamed at what I had done, and I really thought that he was going to ream me out, laugh at me, or tell me how stupid I was.

"But without preaching at me, he showed me the mistakes I made, and then he gave me some ideas of things that I could do to pull myself out of that mess. He warned me that it wasn't going to be a quick fix.

Nothing that lasts ever is. And I was starting out with less than what I had started out from before."

He paused for a moment, thinking back on that hard, difficult, agonizing conversation. "He also highly recommended that I pay everyone everything I owed, with interest. He said that he knew that I had borrowed some money from friends, and that included him, and that the friends would understand if I couldn't pay them back. Especially the ones that were rich enough to not notice. But he told me a man's only as good as his word. And I knew that."

"And yet you didn't keep your word to me." Becky might have been trying to keep the bitterness out of her voice, but she was not successful.

"No. I didn't keep my word to you. And the longer it went that I didn't keep my word, the worse I felt about it, and the harder it was for me to face the idea of facing you. And I kept telling myself that it would be easier when I had money, and then when I finally got things to turn around, I continued to tell myself that. Like more money would somehow make a difference. Like I could eventually have enough money that I would look strong and invincible in your eyes. And... I just kept putting it off. I guess I was scared more than anything. But my excuses sounded legitimate in my mind."

"I see."

He wasn't sure whether she really did or not. She wasn't a man, and she didn't understand a man's need to...look strong? Like a provider, like someone who could protect, someone who could be counted on. Obviously, if he lost everything, he couldn't be counted on for anything.

They didn't talk much more as they continued on the highway. He thought maybe Becky had fallen asleep, and he didn't want to say anything that might wake her up. Thankfully the babies slept, but by the time they pulled into the apartment, it was late, and they were crying again.

"We're home," he said softly.

Becky stirred and then sat up with an abrupt, "oof!"

She looked around. "Did I sleep that long?"

"I guess you must've. But it sounds like Marley or Kevin, or maybe both of them are awake in the back seat."

"Wow. I'm sorry. I could have fed them if you would have woken me up."

"You know, sometimes we sleep best in cars, for some reason."

"Yeah. I was very deeply asleep. But I feel better," she said, looking over and smiling at him.

"You sound better too," he said. "Would you unlock the door, and I'll carry the babies in? You can get started making bottles?"

"Sounds good."

He handed over the key, which he'd grabbed on the way out. It was her sister's apartment, but he supposed that the keys were his responsibility. He didn't care. He was just glad she was allowing him to help. She could kick him out. Or divide the time so each of them had the babies for a certain amount of time.

He was getting attached to them though, and the idea of that was less and less appealing. How did actual parents do that? Allow their child to just be taken from their home and into someone else's home, even if the person taking them was the other parent?

He hoped he never had to find out, because that seemed like it would be exceptionally difficult and painful.

Twenty

Two days later, Becky stood at the casket of her sister, greeting the last of the mourners. When Mr. Carson had been at their apartment, he had called the church in Raspberry Ridge specifically to find out if it would be okay to have the service there.

Of course Pastor Miller had been fine with it and agreed to do the service.

He didn't really know Rita, who had moved out of Raspberry Ridge a decade prior, but Becky appreciated him doing it anyway.

It was a cold, windy day, gray skies, perfect for her mood, with the threat of snow looming.

The babies were tucked snugly in their car seats, and Rodney had told her he would take care of anything that needed to be done with them so that she could focus on talking to people and dealing with her grief.

She had been surprised at the turnout. She hadn't been expecting so many people. Maybe that was what happened when a person died young, or maybe Rita was more beloved than what she thought. Just because she was a foster girl, who had officially been adopted by a family in Strawberry Sands, didn't mean that she didn't have family, she supposed.

Still, when a person was older when they were adopted, sometimes it was hard to feel connected to the family.

Becky felt unmoored, like the one person in the world she belonged to was no longer there. Not that she didn't love the family who adopted her and treated her like their own.

And not that Rodney didn't hold a place in her heart too. Probably, of all the people left in the world, he was the one who made her feel the most like she wasn't just going to drift away, since she had no one to tie her to earth anymore.

The last of the mourners gave her a hug, which she returned. And then she took one last look at her sister, who looked so peaceful, almost as though she were just sleeping. Then they closed the casket, moved it to the back of the church, and the service started.

Seeing the casket close was exceptionally difficult for Becky. She couldn't help but think that it would never open again. That her sister didn't like the dark. Back when Rita was little, Becky spent more than a few nights in her bed, holding her crying sister who just wanted to have a light turned on.

Whatever foster family they were staying with at the time wouldn't allow it.

Eventually they were separated, and Becky wasn't there to comfort her. She had promised when she had run away from her foster family just to be able to see her sister that she would never allow them to be separated again. Yet here she was. The casket was closed, and her sister was going to be wheeled away. There was already a grave dug in the old churchyard.

She would be lowered into the ground, and Becky would never see her again. It felt like she was abdicating her responsibilities as an older sister, even though, logically, she knew that her sister was not in that body anymore.

Still, it was hard to see it go. Hard to know that this was the last time she would lay eyes on that earthly body. Hard.

Her heart ached and wasn't even broken; it was damaged beyond repair. Her chest hurt, but she wouldn't allow herself to cry. She sat stoically, not listening to the pastor, just telling herself that she could get through. She would hold on until it was over, and then she would leave.

There was going to be no graveside service because of the weather. She didn't want people to be out in the blowing wind and the snow and tramping through the ice, and the night before, she'd had a nightmare about someone slipping and falling into the waiting grave.

The thought jerked her awake, and she'd sat up straight on the couch where she'd fallen asleep after getting Kevin up and feeding him. As she looked over, Rodney had been sitting on the recliner with Marley lying on her stomach on his chest. She could see Marley's little face, with her mouth open, and her back going up and down.

As she looked, Rodney had opened one eye. He was dozing but awake. Marley was safe, cradled in his strong hands, and she felt safe too.

It almost felt like they were a family, and having him in her eyesight after the horror of her dream had calmed her heart rate and enabled her to go almost directly back to sleep.

Soon, the service was over, and Becky stood and thanked the people around her for coming. She tried not to pay attention as the casket was wheeled out, and the pallbearers carried it to the hearse.

Mr. Carson came over and put a hand on her shoulder. "Would you like to ride along while we take your sister to the cemetery?"

She wanted to say yes, and she looked over at Rodney, who had both babies in his arms and was bouncing them.

They had gotten fussy during the service, but she barely noticed, and she certainly hadn't offered to help. She felt bad now, but he looked more than capable.

She lifted her brows. He couldn't have had any idea what she was asking, but he nodded his head. As though to tell her that whatever she needed to do, he had the babies and he was good. She didn't need to worry about it.

She looked at Mr. Carson. "Please. I'd appreciate that." Not only did she want to, but it would get her away from all of these people. They meant well, they truly did, and she appreciated the fact that they were here, showing support, paying respect to her sister, and it was gratifying to know that so many people cared. But she wanted to be alone. She needed to be alone.

Mr. Carson put a hand on her back and guided her down the aisle.

She hadn't been to too many funerals, and she wasn't sure what was supposed to happen after this. Maybe a meal? She hadn't even thought about a meal. Maybe the next funeral she planned she could remember that, and then she almost choked on her laughter. She couldn't laugh at the end of her sister's funeral. She didn't want to ever, ever have to plan another funeral.

If she and Rodney got together, she might have to plan his eventually.

That wasn't a reason to avoid getting together with someone, was it? Because one wanted to avoid planning any more funerals in their lifetime?

She wasn't sure. It seemed like a pretty legitimate reason to her. But the idea of telling Rodney that she never wanted to see him again was… too hard. She had eighteen years. He'd be around for eighteen years, he had said. She could count on that.

With that thought, she walked out into the cold, late February day and got in the passenger seat of the hearse as Mr. Carson held the door for her.

She was going to say goodbye to her sister. And she was going to do it alone.

Twenty-One

It was another late night as Rodney pulled into the parking lot of Rita's apartment. He had expected it to be, and Becky had again fallen asleep. It was like the night they had come home from looking at the house. Only this time, he left the car running and tried not to wake her as he got the babies up, carefully unhooking them and carrying them in. Neither one of them were awake either. He set them down softly.

He had both babies in, and he wondered what to do with Becky.

Just let her sleep in the car? Should he wake her up?

Or should he try to carry her?

He had been a regular at the gym a few weeks ago before his life imploded. He didn't mean imploded. Imploded implied something bad. He felt like his life had taken a turn for the better, but it had changed abruptly, and he hardly recognized any of what it was like now, compared to what it had been.

Suffice it to say, he hadn't been to the gym in several weeks, but Becky had always been small, and that hadn't changed. So, while he thought she would probably prefer that he not carry her in and just wake her up, he decided that he was going to try.

He opened her door softly and reached over, shutting the car off and unbuckling her belt at the same time.

She stirred a little, and he murmured, "I'm going to carry you in. We're home."

"Huh?" she said sleepily.

"I'm putting my arms under your legs and around your shoulders. If you can hold onto me, that would be helpful."

"Rodney?" she asked, softly, like she didn't know where she was or who he was.

"Yeah. It's me. I'm going to carry you into the house. It's okay. The babies are already in there."

"We're home?" she asked, sounding confused.

"Yes. I've got you. You're safe."

"I know. I'm always safe with you." She snuggled deeper into his arms as he straightened and closed the door. He felt her warm breath on his neck and wished the apartment was a mile away so he could hold her that long.

But by the time he got up the steps and maneuvered her in the door, he thought that a mile might have been a touch too much.

Still, he could make it to the couch and sit down with her.

She was awake, he could tell the difference in her breathing, but she hadn't lifted her head and stayed snuggled against him. Almost as though she needed it. She'd come back from burying her sister, and to her surprise, and his as well, the church had planned a meal. Neither one of them had known about it, but they had stayed, eating and listening to people reminisce about the girls when they were younger. It was nice to be around so many people who knew them and see their perspective of the things he remembered.

Becky and he had been together so much, but a lot of it had been out of the eyes of the townspeople. Especially in their younger years.

Regardless, it had been late when they had left, and the ride home was brutal.

Hopefully his lawyer would have some information about the house soon, and they would be closing. He had honestly expected to hear from the lawyer today.

He walked by the babies, both of whom just had their faces peeking out from the covers that went over their car seats. He'd pulled a little flap down when he'd set them on the floor so that he could see them. He also had them pointed toward the couch and the recliner, because he assumed that that's where Becky and he were going to end up.

But rather than lay Becky on the couch, he sat down, holding her in his arms.

She snuggled deeper.

"I'm just going to sit here for a bit," he said. His boots were still on, and so were her shoes, and he probably should take both of those things off, as well as her coat and get her settled properly. But he just wanted to hold her. She was lighter than he expected, and much skinnier. Almost too skinny to be called slender. It made him wonder again what her financial situation had been lately, and he'd never remembered to ask.

Or if he had, she hadn't given him a satisfactory answer. He determined to press her in the morning, although he supposed it didn't matter. She had been letting him take care of her, and that was the thing that was important to him right now.

He settled down on the couch and waited for her breathing to even out. Then, he grabbed the blanket that was behind them and settled it over top of them.

The babies were going to be up soon. They hadn't eaten since they left Raspberry Ridge, and it was just a matter of time. Neither one of them were even close to sleeping through the night. What had it been? A week? Ten days? More or less? Not that it mattered, but he had lost track of time.

All he knew was that he had Becky right where he wanted her, and he wished that they could stay this way forever.

He was just going to enjoy it for a little while.

Twenty-Two

Becky woke to both babies screaming at the top of their lungs. Kevin still made a cute mewing sound, even when he was crying, but Marley's cry changed into something that was shrill and demanding.

Either way, it sounded like they had been crying for a while by the time she finally struggled out of the depths of unconsciousness and tried to figure out where and how she was. She didn't feel normal. She felt...a little uncomfortable. Her neck ached, but she felt warm and safe and snuggled up, and it was weird, because she had just come from the funeral of her sister, and she shouldn't be feeling this good.

And then she realized that Rodney held her. She vaguely remembered he carried her in and sat on the couch. She had thought that she needed to get up and take her shoes off and her coat and check on the babies, but the next thing she knew, she had been deeply asleep.

"I can get them. You lie down." His words were soft in her ears, his breath over her skin, and her arms were already around him, but she wanted to move them up, to slide her fingers in his hair and bring his head down to hers.

But that wouldn't do with the babies crying.

"No. I'll... I'll make the bottles."

That was what she was supposed to do. She wasn't sure where the baby bags were, or whether he had even gotten the dirty bottles out, but she was pretty sure they'd made sure that there were clean bottles at the sink before they left, anticipating the needs that might arise when they got home.

Plus, there were extra clean bottles in the baby bags. They had been figuring out that whatever they thought they needed, they should double it.

That included the number of diapers that they took anywhere and the number of outfit changes too.

Although, really the only place they had gone was to look at the house, and now her sister's funeral. The babies were so young, and she really liked to keep them at home. She thought that was best for them. Although soon, this wouldn't be home anymore.

She moved, reluctantly sliding off his lap and standing up. Taking a moment to orient herself before realizing that the blanket had slipped to the floor.

She grabbed it and threw it over the back of the couch, then turned around to offer her hand to him.

"My arm's asleep," he said.

"I'm sorry," she murmured.

"No. I... I enjoyed it."

She didn't say anything but continued to hold her hand out until he grabbed it, and she helped him up.

He had said something about still wanting to be with her. But she didn't know exactly what that meant. He had abruptly cut off their relationship, and she didn't know whether when he said that he wanted to be with her, he meant until something else happened that he was going to not want to tell her, or whether it meant this time for real.

She knew he wanted her to believe that it meant this time for real, but... How did she go about doing that?

She walked over to the counter, pulling two clean bottles from the rack, and started to get them ready for Rodney, who had knelt down beside one of the car seats and was opening it up. He would get a diaper changed while she made the bottle.

She realized she was still wearing her coat, so she took it off and threw it on the stool.

She was wearing her boots as well, but they would just have to wait. The babies were crying in earnest now, and she would get them taken care of first. If she worked, she would have both bottles almost ready when he had one diaper changed, and she would feed the first twin while he changed the second diaper. They kind of had a system going. Whoever started changing the diapers just did them both.

Neither one of them fussed or complained about getting the short end of the stick. They were past that, she thought. Or maybe both of them were willing to do whatever work it took.

She screwed on the last bottle's cap and carried them both over to the coffee table where Rodney had just finished changing one of the babies. In the dark, she couldn't tell which one. Thank goodness they were different genders, otherwise she probably would get them mixed up and never be able to figure out which one was which.

He handed the baby to her, carefully cradling its head.

"This is Marley." He grinned. "She's the loudest."

The other baby was still crying, and Marley was still making angry whimpering sounds.

"The squeaky wheel and all that," she said, feeling more awake and a little bit embarrassed at how she had been sleeping.

He seemed fine, totally comfortable. Like it wasn't any big deal.

But it was a big deal to her. She didn't do that with just anyone. In fact, she didn't do it with anyone.

But Rodney was different. She didn't mind doing it with Rodney. Once upon a time, she dreamed every night about kissing him.

He was definitely her teenage crush, and her young adult crush, and her now crush apparently, because she found herself sitting down on the couch, watching him work. Admiring him.

Had he really abandoned the opportunity to become even richer? Selling off what he had to come back here to take care of babies?

What did that say about him?

And he seemed to indicate that he was going to stay. He said he was arranging things, getting rid of the staff and all that, buying a house in Raspberry Ridge. That sure looked like a man who meant what he said about sticking around.

She'd been burned by him once.

But for the years and years before that, decade even, he had done everything he said he was going to. Was she going to hold just one little mistake against him?

It was a five-year mistake. He could have corrected it anytime, and he didn't.

But he explained why, and it did make sense. Yeah, she didn't really understand the man's need to look all macho and all that, but she understood that it was there.

Kind of like her need to look pretty and go shopping, or even her need to see the future and at least have an idea of what was there so she could make plans and adjust her schedule accordingly.

It really wasn't necessary. The Bible told them to live day by day. And not to worry, because God would take care of them.

He finished changing the diaper and carefully set the baby in one of the car seats while he went and washed his hands.

They really needed to get bassinets or beds or something. But before they did that, they should see how long it was going to take to get the house in Raspberry Ridge. It didn't make any sense to load this house up with stuff, only to carry everything up there.

Cart and horse and all that, she thought to herself.

He came back, sat down, grabbed the bottle, and carefully picked up the baby.

Kevin was crying almost as loud as Marley usually did by the time Rodney leaned back and put the bottle in his mouth.

Kevin took a moment to realize what happened, and then a blissful quiet descended on the living room.

"Well. That feels better," Rodney said, sounding relieved but also a tone of humor in his voice.

"Yeah. So much better."

"How long until they sleep through the night?" he asked.

She thought it might have been a rhetorical question. "I haven't looked. But I think it varies. Anywhere from two months to a year or later."

"Two months? We've got another...nine weeks of this?"

"Seven weeks. And maybe our babies will be early."

"They're smaller than regular babies. Do you think that means that they'll be earlier or later?"

"Probably later."

"Wow. The idea of doing this for another seven weeks makes me want to...cry, I guess. That's probably my biggest urge right now."

She looked at him. He hadn't shed a tear during the funeral. He looked sad, he looked grave, and he'd even looked concerned about her a few times. But there had been no crying.

She normally didn't cry either. And she hadn't cried during the funeral. She hadn't even cried at the graveside, although she felt like it. It wasn't as deserted as what she thought. There were the workers, and several pallbearers had come along so they could carry the casket to the grave.

"Thank you for being there today. Thank you for your support and your care. I wasn't expecting that, and it really touched me. This was probably one of the hardest things I've ever done in my life before, and you were right there with me ready to give me anything I needed. I appreciate it."

The words as they came out of her mouth were sincere, and she meant them with all of her heart.

He sat there, his eyes dark as his head leaned back on the edge of the couch, watching her. His smile was a little sad as he met her eyes, then he looked down.

"I'm glad I was there. I wouldn't have wanted you to have done that by yourself. I...don't want you to ever have to do anything by yourself. It's always better if you have someone who loves you with you."

There he went, talking about love again, and she wasn't sure that she was ready for that. Not yet. But she did think that she was more ready now than she had been. Because after all, he'd shown her today that he meant what he was saying, that he would be there for her and support her. And he didn't seem to act like he wanted to be somewhere else. So many times, she'd seen men who were bored or impatient or didn't care to be where they were, and yet... Rodney seemed to just want to be wherever she was. And he was content as long as she was there.

That's the way she felt about him. As long as he was there, she was happy. Would she have been happy in the business world?

She figured she probably would have been. She wouldn't have wanted to sell her horses for it, but now they were gone, she wasn't getting them back, and... Maybe there was more to life than horses anyway. Maybe she had put too much stock in her horses, and while they had been such great friends, they were expensive friends. They hadn't really made any money for her. All they had been was a lot of work and a lot of expenses, and she had to get other jobs, just to buy their feed and pay for their care.

Of course, she hadn't really known how to advertise her business either. And that was part of the problem. In order to advertise, one had to have money, and if one wasn't good at advertising, one could lose a lot of money that they never got back.

She'd lost some and then been afraid to lose more.

"What are you thinking about?" he asked, his voice sounding tired yet curious.

She yelped out a laugh. "Isn't that my question?"

"Men aren't supposed to want to know what women are thinking, right?" he said, grinning sheepishly. "I really want to know."

"All right. I was thinking about my horses."

"You regret selling them?"

"Probably no more than you regret selling the part of the business you sold to Ford Hansen."

"I don't regret that at all."

"All right. Maybe a little more than that. Because I don't regret it, exactly. And I would do it again in a heartbeat. It's not like I'm wishing I could go back and undo it."

"I have things like that in my life. Things I wish I could go back and undo."

"Well, me too, but not this. I'm confident I did the right thing. But... I am going to miss them." She was quiet for a minute as Marley finished her bottle and turned her face to the side. Her eyes closed, and she looked like she had fallen asleep again. She couldn't sleep yet. She hadn't burped. So, Becky flipped her over and started patting her back.

"Are you gonna try to buy them back?" he asked softly.

"No. I was thinking that I wouldn't have wanted to sell them, but now that they're gone, I guess... That opens up new doors for me. You know? Like, while the horses were there, I was kind of tied to Raspberry Ridge. I couldn't go anywhere because they needed to be fed morning and night. Or I needed to put them out to pasture, then make sure they didn't get out. Or I had bookings I had to be there for. But now, I don't have those things to tie me down. I can maybe do something else. I actually had to get another job to help pay for their feed and...maybe I would have money to buy, oh, I don't know, something." She couldn't really think of anything she wanted. Other than enough food. She wouldn't mind if she never ate beans and rice again.

"So...what are you thinking you want to do?"

"I was just thinking I was pretty content here. And I was wondering if you wanted to go back to your business."

"I am pretty content here too. I was thinking that this evening while you were sleeping. The babies were sleeping, and I was almost asleep but awake enough to appreciate the fact that it felt like I had a family. And... It's been a long time since I felt like I belonged to a family." He just left it at that. He had parents, but the horrific murder-suicide had practically erased the few good childhood memories he'd had. He was so grateful to the Landry brothers and their wives who had taken him under their wing and made sure he healed from that trauma.

"Yeah. I guess that's what this feeling inside of me is. It feels pretty good. Wish my sister could have felt it."

"I think maybe she did a little bit while she was pregnant. Did you notice that she just seemed to glow with contentment when you saw her? Or maybe that was just the evening I saw her. She seemed so happy."

"No, you're right. She did seem to have a glow about her, even though she looked terrible. I guess on the one hand, I'm not surprised she didn't make it through the operation. I'm only surprised she didn't die earlier. Because she looked awful. But she did have a glow about her. Just a satisfaction and peace. And I think she was happy."

"She had these babies growing in her. Her perfect family right in her body."

"She never complained that the father didn't want to have anything to do with them."

"I don't think she needed him to."

She hadn't wanted his name on the birth certificate or wanted him to have anything to do with them, and he hadn't shown any interest. Which was sad. The idea that a dad didn't want anything to do with his child. How could he create another human being and just walk away from it? Part of his body, his lineage, and not even care?

She couldn't get that. It didn't make any sense at all to her.

"All right. Marley gave me one good burp, and I'm going to try to put her down."

She leaned forward, able to get Marley into the car seat, settling her in, tucking her little blanket around her, not too snuggly, because it wasn't chilly in the apartment. And she didn't want Marley to get too hot.

She made sure she was safely enclosed before she leaned back on the couch.

She should move to the recliner so she could lie down, and then Rodney could have the couch when Kevin was done eating.

Normally she got it, but it really didn't seem fair that she got the most comfortable piece of furniture all the time. It was only right that he would get to have it once in a while.

But she was content where she was, tired, and she didn't want to move.

"You never took your boots off," he said, smiling a bit.

"Did you take yours off?" she asked.

"I'm going to. I assumed I was going to get to sleep a little after this, and I don't typically sleep with my boots on."

"Is it going to bother you if I sleep with mine on? I'm so tired I'm not sure I have the energy to take them off."

She hadn't realized that he'd moved and must have put Kevin in his car seat, because the next thing she knew, he was kneeling in front of her, unlacing her boots and sliding them off.

"Oh my goodness. You don't have to do that," she said, but it was all she could do to get the energy to talk.

"I know. But I want to. You'll be more comfortable this way."

"I'll be more comfortable if you hold me the way you did earlier. I haven't slept that well in a really long time."

"It might just be because you're so exhausted you can sleep anywhere. You were pretty sound asleep in the car."

"I guess you're right. But...there was something comforting about sleeping with you." His heartbeat under her ear made her feel safe and protected. But there was also shared intimacy that came from holding onto another human. And not just another random human, but someone she knew and loved and respected and whom she knew admired and respected her as well.

He didn't say anything else, and she wasn't paying attention as he slipped his boots off and stood up.

Then, to her surprise, he sat down on the other side of her, between the end of the couch and where she was sitting, and put his arm around her.

"We can't make a habit of this, but for one night, it won't hurt anything."

No. It wouldn't hurt anything for one night, and she was so tired, she couldn't think straight anyway. So, she snuggled closer, putting her arm around his waist and burrowing her head in his chest.

His arm came around her waist, and she pressed against his thigh. Perfect. This was exactly the way she wanted to spend the rest of her life.

If only she knew he wouldn't ditch her again.

Twenty-Three

Rodney and Becky got up one other time in the middle of the night to feed the babies. He knew that it would make more sense if one of them did the nightly feedings every other night so one of them got to sleep through the night. But he liked getting up when it was dark and quiet and still, he liked murmuring with Becky and the cozy feeling of being the only two adults in the world, with their babies and them being in this dark cocoon together.

He loved holding her, and after they fed the babies again, they snuggled in the same way.

He knew he shouldn't. This was where he got into trouble before. This was why he had a woman messaging his lawyer, demanding money.

Not that he was afraid Becky would do that. He was afraid that he would step outside the bounds of what was right. It was better to have guardrails up to keep himself from doing anything even remotely wrong in the first place. One of those guardrails for him was he didn't stay overnight in a woman's house. Ever. For anything.

Except when he made a promise to her dying sister on her deathbed that he'd take care of the sister's twin babies with the woman he couldn't stop thinking about, couldn't stop loving, no matter how hard he tried.

Yes. He was in a mess. And he couldn't just leave. He had not explained to Becky why he couldn't stay all night anymore.

He was awake at six o'clock with Kevin, who was fussing, and he managed to get out from underneath Becky without her waking up and then pick up Kevin and walk the floor with him a little bit.

By seven, he had a message from his lawyer.

Again, a message this early in the morning couldn't be good news, so he shifted Kevin in the crook of one arm, settled him down a little bit, and opened the message.

> The woman who is trying to extort money out of you by saying she has a child by you said that she would agree to your terms, but you had to meet with her. I have the agreement her lawyer sent over, and I looked over it. It says what she said it was going to, that you owe so much money, and as long as you pay that, she'll give up all rights to the baby. The only condition she has is that you meet with her first. If you agree to this, you can sign the agreement, send it back, and I will facilitate the meeting.

Wow.

Rodney took a deep breath; he wasn't sure what to say. That was... maybe easier than what he thought it was going to be, but he felt bad. Why was she so easily giving up her rights to the child? Was his son going to be upset about that? How would he feel about not seeing his mom again?

There was no way he was going to know unless he met with Stella. So, it was a no-brainer.

Thankfully, he had to bring his printer from the office to print some other things off, so he had it set up on the counter.

He hit print before he realized that it might wake the girls up.

As it printed, Becky stirred.

He thought about canceling the print job, but it was almost done. It was a simple agreement, only two pages long, and by the time he got it back up on his phone to cancel it, it was done.

Kevin had fallen asleep in his arms, so he set the agreement on the counter and then walked back over to the car seat and set him inside.

"Good morning," Becky said sleepily, smiling at him a little.

He couldn't resist. She had pushed up, and the place where he'd been all night was empty, so he glided around the car seat and sat back down, putting his arm around her and pressing his lips to her forehead.

"Good morning, beautiful."

He heard her breathy chuckle, and her hand came over and wrapped around his stomach.

His muscles clenched involuntarily and then relaxed. It felt good to have her touch on him. He wished she did it more.

"I could get used to snuggling with you all night," Becky said softly.

"I could get used to it too," he said simply. He wanted to tell her that it was up to her, because he was willing to do whatever it took to make sure that they were never separated again. He wanted marriage, which was what he always wanted with Becky..

"I'm sorry I was holding everything against you. I realized last night that I was basically expecting you to be perfect and was allowing one little mistake to stand between us."

There wasn't just one mistake. But she didn't know that. "It was a five-year mistake."

That is true, and she would agree.

"But it's not really, you know? I've probably made mistakes that people overlook, and that made it so that I was able to get past them. But they could have snowballed. Like, for example, when I ran away from that first foster care family. If you hadn't been willing to take me in, if you hadn't helped me eat, it could have been a mistake that changed my life for the worst. I could have fallen in with the wrong kind of people, you know?" She took a breath. "If you had been a different kind of person," she said softly.

He assumed that she was saying that he could have taken advantage of her.

"You were pretty little those first few years, and I just thought you were a kid, but I noticed when you started to grow up. That was part of the reason I needed to leave."

There had been so many years between them that it would have been dangerous for them to have been together. Illegal.

She stretched and yawned. "It's pretty early for you to be doing business, especially considering that you told me that you weren't going to be doing much business anymore. What's on the counter?"

Her hand went around his waist again, and she snuggled her head into his shoulder, curling herself up against him, and he closed his eyes, wanting to growl in frustration.

Now? Now was when she was going to ask him?

He ran his hand down her hair and another one over her shoulder and down her arm, finding her fingers and threading them together.

"There's one other thing that I've been hesitating telling you about, because I was afraid you would hate me even more than you already did."

"I never hated you. And I can't imagine that there's anything you could tell me that would make me hate you."

She might not hate him, but she would be really, really disappointed in him.

But she asked. And he told himself that when she asked, he was going to tell her. It seemed like now was the time.

"When everything imploded, I lost it all. I declared bankruptcy, I told you about it."

"Yeah. I remember. It's okay. No one would have thought less of you. So you took a risk. So you lost. It's like a quarterback taking a risk in throwing to the receiver with double coverage, who's got a straight shot to the end zone, rather than the single covered receiver that has two defenders behind him. Both of them are risks, I suppose."

"Wow. I didn't know you knew so much about football."

He was distracted for a moment, or maybe he just was putting off the inevitable.

"Rick made me watch a couple of times. He was mostly into trucks and motors and that type of thing, but he did spend some weekends in front of the TV set screaming at guys running around chasing a ball, and I figured I ought to try to understand it a little more than just rolling my eyes at grown men caring so much about where a ball was."

He laughed. Leave it to Becky to talk about football like that.

He wanted to procrastinate, to change the subject, but he needed to face this. It was a relief in a way. "Anyway. I told you I lost my lease on my apartment because I couldn't pay."

"Yeah." She said that easily, like it didn't bother her at all.

Now, he wished he would have just told her. It would have kept this next part from happening. But what happened next was part of his past. And it would always be that way.

His stomach knotted, and he felt his hands sweating, although he didn't let go of her fingers. He didn't tighten his grip though. Because he figured she would be pulling away shortly.

"I told you I stayed with a friend."

"Yeah."

"That friend was a girl."

He could feel the change in her. Feel that she kind of had an idea now. Feel her pull in, just a bit. He continued before she could say anything.

"That girl, Stella was her name. She had a one-bedroom apartment. She told me I could sleep on the couch. I was grateful to not be on the street, because that's where I thought I was going to be. Anyway, there were men who moved in and out. She hooked up pretty often, I guess is what you call it. And I was on the couch. One weekend, she didn't have anyone to hook up with, and she...hooked up with me."

That was a disgusting way to say it, but it was the truth.

Becky had gone completely still, and even though her hand still lay in his, it almost grew colder as he held it.

"You gonna say anything?" he asked.

"I'm waiting for the rest of the story. Is there more?" she asked, and her voice was small, and it sounded like it hurt. Like there was pain that was coming from her bones and oozing out her voice.

"I guess there were two other times where she didn't have a date, if that's what you call it, and she turned to me. I...had zero experience, and I couldn't have been a good hookup in hindsight. But I went along with it. I guess I just felt bad about myself, whatever. There's no excuse for it. By the third time, I knew it was going to continue unless I did something. That's when I found that apartment that I told you about.

The cheapest thing I could find, in the worst and most dangerous section of Chicago. Anything to get out of there. That's what I did. I didn't have much, just three suits and some T-shirts and jeans. I took them with me and moved out. And I thought that was it."

"It wasn't?" she asked, and while her voice was a little louder, it still held that note of pain or betrayal or whatever it was. She deserved to feel it all. She deserved to have every piece of her anger directed against him. He couldn't sense any right now, but he was sure it was coming. It was inevitable. How could she not be angry with him?

"I thought it was. I thought that was the end of it. I didn't see her, didn't talk to her. It wasn't like there were any kind of emotional attachments. She just...didn't like to be alone on the weekends, I guess. I don't know. I don't really understand that mentality, and I knew that wasn't the person I wanted to be. No matter how financially devastated I was, I didn't have to be morally devastated either. Although...it's too late to get back what I don't have any more."

He paused for a moment, not wanting to dwell on that but trying to figure out how to say the rest. "Anyway. Not long ago, my lawyer was contacted by a lawyer that she had hired. Stella. Now remember, when we hooked up," he cringed over the words, "I had nothing. Literally nothing. I was bumming out on her couch, and I didn't even have money to give her for food. So, she must have seen me somewhere and realized I now had money, and the note from her lawyer said that she had a son, and she wanted compensation."

"Oh my goodness," Becky breathed.

"Yeah," he finally said. Then he wished he wouldn't have said it, because she pushed up and away from him and moved over to the other side of the couch, bringing her legs up to her chest and hugging them, facing him.

Her hair was messed up, her face red from leaning on him, and her eyes red rimmed from the funeral and being up with the babies the night before, and maybe they were filling with tears now, he couldn't tell.

He watched her as he said, "I was aghast. It was not that long ago, and it was after I had seen you. You were all I thought about. You were the only one I ever wanted. Ever. Everything I did, I did it for you. I did it all with us in mind. Our future. I just knew you would always be loyal to me. There was never any question in my mind about that. Even though I didn't talk to you. I didn't worry about that at all."

He didn't mean to make her feel guilty, but her face changed, like she knew she hadn't been loyal, and she looked down.

"I'm not knocking you. I'm just telling you how I felt. There was never a doubt in my mind that you and I were going to be together. I meant every word, everything I ever wrote to you. It was all true. And then, I got this thing from my lawyer, knowing that I had a child. And that was after I saw you again, and I knew I needed to tell you what had happened and why I hadn't talked to you and tried to make things right, and then this big bombshell dropped in my lap."

"And what did you do?" she asked, and he didn't know how she would react to this. But he hoped he had done the right thing.

"I told my lawyer that I would pay it. Whatever she asked, and the only thing I wanted in return was for her to give up all of her rights and to give me full custody."

Becky's eyes got big, and her mouth opened, and then she said, "But what if the little boy is attached to his mother? You're going to rip his mother away from him?"

"I don't know. I guess. I... I didn't know what to do. I just knew I didn't want to co-parent with Stella. Someone I barely knew and shouldn't have been with. Anyway, what's lying on the counter over there is her lawyer's response to my request. She's agreed to it, as long as I agree to meet with her just one time. I need to sign it and send it back to my lawyer, and my lawyer will facilitate a meeting between us, and I'll find out what she's going to say."

"You can't take a little boy from his mother."

He didn't say anything for a moment, and then he said, "I wondered if she was even raising the child. Maybe she has her mother doing it or someone else, but you're right. I don't want to step in and upend his world, but at the same time, I don't want my child to be raised by a bunch of strangers, who do drugs while he's playing with his toys on the floor in front of them."

Becky nodded and seemed to be able to understand what he was saying as he said that, and she didn't argue with him anymore.

"Honestly, I'm not sure the boy's mine. She said she had a paternity test done, and he is mine, but I don't know how she would have done that. I never donated any DNA for any tests." He still wasn't sure. She could have taken it from him while he was at her apartment, but that would have been showing a lot of foresight and patience.

"You said she had been hooking up every weekend?"

"Yeah. Every weekend, she was with someone. Usually someone different. I think I saw a couple of guys come around a few times, but... sometimes she was with one guy Saturday evening and went to bed with someone else the next night. It was...kinda gross."

"Yeah. Ouch. That's gross and sad." Becky hesitated. "So, you're going to meet with her?"

"Yeah. As soon as my lawyer sets up the meeting." He paused and then said, "Do you want to go?"

Her eyes opened big, and then she tilted her head as though she were thinking about it. "Yeah. I think I would."

It was his turn to be surprised. She didn't seem to be overly angry. In fact, he was hard-pressed to detect any anger at all, and...he definitely wasn't expecting her to want to go meet with Stella.

"I don't understand why you're not angry with me."

Her brows drew down, and she tucked her legs closer to her, drawing them to her and putting her chin on them. "I'm not sure. But I don't feel anger. I just feel...sad. Maybe a little empty. I definitely pity Stella. The idea that that's a good life to someone. How little you must value yourself to hook up with anyone and everyone. Whoever's available. That's just kinda hard to wrap my head around. Maybe that's overshadowing everything, but... I suppose the idea that you moved out. That you went to someplace dangerous and hard, that you knew that what you were doing was wrong, I don't know. It's kind of hurtful that you did it while you weren't talking to me, but it would have been worse if you had done it while you and I were still talking, you know?"

He didn't really understand why something would have been worse. He thought she would be a lot more angry at him having sex with another woman than she would have been at him not talking to her for five years, but maybe she was just tired of being angry. Maybe she was just tired of being disappointed in him.

Or maybe it was a delayed reaction, and when she thought about it for a while, then she would be angry.

"Regardless. I'm sorry. I have always loved you. And I know I always will. Being with you is like coming home. It feels right. Nothing else does." He realized as he was saying it that it was the absolute truth. Nothing else felt just right like being with Becky. She had the ability to make him feel like he was home.

"That's how I feel about you. I guess it took me a little while to figure that out. But that's exactly the way I feel. Being with you is like being home. And I don't want to trade it for anything." She paused for a moment, and then she said, "And I don't want to get unreasonably angry at you for making mistakes. Especially at mistakes you made five years ago." She paused, then looked at him. "Is there anything else you aren't telling me?"

He laughed. "No. No other women. Not even close. I learned my lesson with that, and I have a couple of ladies that I work with, but I have an office that is completely glass. Every wall. There's a bathroom, but it just has a toilet in it. There is definitely no room for any kind of, well, I suppose people could make room for what they want to make room for, but I promise you, for me, doing anything in that bathroom besides using the toilet is just gross, okay?"

She laughed. "I believe you. I've had to think about things since the babies were born. You never lie to me. I mean, you might have made promises that you didn't keep, but you never tried to pretend they were something that you didn't say. You might have not wanted to tell me what you were doing, but instead of going completely silent on me, you could have lied to me. There was nothing preventing you from writing letters to me telling me how well you were doing, and how much money you were making, and how you were traveling here or there. But you didn't. You didn't lie. And I guess that means more to me than anything. That shows me that you respect me enough to tell me the truth. And there is something that is sadly sweet about you wanting to look your very best for me. I can respect that."

"Thank you. I wasn't sure that you would ever understand."

"It took me a little while. Sometimes I can be slow."

"Oh, Beckpet. You are a lot of things, but slow is not one of them."

She laughed with him. And then he said, "Do you think that we could handle another kid?" He looked at the two car seats, quiet for now, but that had been a huge adjustment. "Bringing a three-and-a-half-year-old boy into the mix would be...crazy."

"We have to handle what we have to handle. Good thing we bought a big house."

She said "we." That made his heart smile.

"Becky?"

"Yeah?" she asked, lifting her brows.

"Maybe this is not a good time to bring this up, but remember how I said I didn't want to live with you?"

"I understand now."

"I want to marry you."

He was surprised when she didn't hesitate, especially considering what he'd just confessed. "All right. That would solve all our problems. And if you're trying to sell yourself, you did a good job of it last night. I could get addicted pretty fast to snuggling with you all night long."

"I'm happy to hear it. Because I'm expecting that as soon as you say 'I do.'"

"All right. You got it," she said.

It was a little awkward for him to move across the couch, but he did anyway, and he took both of her cheeks in his two hands. She moved her knees and leaned closer.

"You know you just agreed to marry me, right?"

"I was hoping that was what that was, because if it wasn't, I was trying to figure out how I was going to propose later today."

"I think we've wasted enough time."

She agreed, nodding.

And then he said, "I've waited a long time to kiss you. I don't think I would have chosen a moment like this, but it feels right. Do you mind?"

"I want you to," she said, putting both hands on his cheeks and pulling his face toward hers.

They shared a sweet, tender, almost bittersweet kiss. One that tasted a little of sadness but mostly of excitement for the new beginnings that they were looking forward to. It wasn't going to be anything like he had thought it was going to be, but he had a feeling it was going to be better. Because anything with Becky was better.

Twenty-Four

It was two weeks until Rodney's lawyer was able to set up a meeting with Stella.

In that amount of time, Rodney and Becky did not sit around. In fact, Becky sometimes wondered if maybe they should have just chilled a little bit more. Because it felt like they were constantly busy and constantly sleep deprived.

But they managed to settle on the house, and they hired people to move the furniture that they'd ordered in, including baby furniture. She and Rodney spent an interesting afternoon trying to get the baby swings put together. It was probably good that they paid someone to assemble the cribs.

They had discussed whether or not they should have the babies in different rooms, and they decided that they would. Even though the hospital had said the twins knew when the other one was close, they were not the same gender, and they were going to have to have separate rooms eventually. They figured that it would be just as easy to do it now as later.

Plus, the house had five bedrooms, so it felt more like they were using it.

They had another bedroom set up, just in case the meeting with

Stella went the way they wanted it to and they ended up with another child.

Becky understood that this child might not even be biologically related to Rodney, but there was no doubt in her mind, and absolutely no hesitation on her part, that the kid needed a home, and they would give him one.

She was sure Stella hadn't bargained on Rodney reacting the way he had, and Becky was interested to see how that meeting went.

She and Rodney had done one other small thing before the day of the meeting arrived.

And that was to get the preacher who had just conducted Rita's funeral to marry them.

It was a small ceremony. Luke and Kristen along with Grif and Chi were able to beam in remotely from their cabin in Alaska. The connection was sketchy, and Becky and Rodney had almost not been able to convince them that they didn't need to cut their trip short. Becky and Rodney agreed that they would have felt terrible if they'd interrupted their trip of a lifetime. The couples already felt bad enough because of missing Rita's funeral, but they'd all promised that when they got back they would be doting on the twins in a massive way.

She felt like they had rushed things a bit, but it made Rodney feel better about sharing the house with her, and it worked for her, too.

She had been a wife for two and a half days when they showed up at the lawyer's office and were escorted into a conference room.

Stella sat there waiting on them.

She turned as they walked in and then partially stood.

"Rodney?" she said, squinting her eyes as though she couldn't believe that the person walking in was the person she remembered.

Rodney had not dressed in a suit and tie for the occasion, but he did look good in a black T-shirt with a sports jacket over it, along with jeans. Becky had enjoyed watching him, and now, she almost smiled at Stella's reaction. Apparently Rodney looked a little different than he had five years ago, and Stella was having trouble reconciling the differences. She should have been expecting someone who looked a little bit prosperous anyway.

Then, she seemed to notice Becky for the first time as the door clicked closed.

"You don't need a lawyer in here with you," she said, eyeing Becky with suspicion and dislike.

"It's my wife, actually. Becky, this is Stella, the girl I told you about. The one who allowed me to stay on her couch for three months. Stella, this is my wife, Becky. The girl I've loved all my life."

"Well, it's interesting that you loved her all your life, but you were having sex with me while you were living in my apartment."

Becky wanted to close her eyes, because it was just crude, and it made her feel dirty somehow. But she lifted her chin and held tight to Rodney's hand.

"I thought you might bring our son along," Rodney said, taking a glance around the room like he might have missed the child sitting somewhere.

They walked to the table and sat down, with Rodney pulling out her chair and Becky smiling her thanks at him.

"So gentlemanly." Stella rolled her eyes.

Rodney ignored her again. "How is he?"

"He's fine. I guess. I haven't seen him for a while. My mom was watching him, but she got sick. I have a friend to keep him for me when I need to do things. A girl needs her space, you know."

Right there, Becky felt better already. The child might be attached to his mother and probably was, but it was obvious that she didn't care about him. Becky wasn't sure she could be any better of a mother, but she did know that she would be there for the child and give him all the love she possibly could. It made her heart sad to think of a little boy growing up without a dad, thinking his dad didn't care about him, and having a mom who just dumped him off on anyone.

"What did you want to talk about?" Rodney asked casually. She admired that he was calm, didn't fall for any of the bait that Stella had thrown out, and had been acting like an adult the entire time. She wanted to remember to tell him how proud of him she was.

"I just couldn't believe that you wanted the kid. You didn't even see him. How do you know I'm not lying?"

"I know we had sex three times. It's quite possible that you might have gotten pregnant. I...didn't have enough experience to have any kind of protection, and I guess I assumed that it was your responsibility. That was my bad."

"Just like that?" She stopped again. "Aren't you going to question me about how I know he's yours?"

"I don't care. I want him. I love him. But I don't want to be dangled around on a string every time you go on a tear. He's either going to be all mine, or I'll see you in court."

The way he said it made a shiver run down Becky's spine. She would have backed down right away. But Stella stopped again.

"Hooray. Whatever. I can't believe you actually want him. But you actually offered me more than what I wanted, and I'd be a fool not to take five million dollars in exchange for the kid. He's done nothing but whine and fuss since he was born." She wrinkled her nose. "Good riddance."

"My lawyer can cut you a check today. How soon can you have the child here?" Rodney asked.

Becky, at that point, was tempted to ask if the child had a name. She was kind of tired of both of them acting like he didn't. But she understood that Rodney was just trying to go along with Stella and was playing the cards he had been dealt.

Stella's eyes lit up at the idea of getting the money that fast. "I can have him for you in an hour."

"All right. The funds are already in my lawyer's account. He can write you out a check as soon as you bring him. As long as you sign the papers stating that you're giving up all of your maternal rights."

"No problem. I'll be right back. Don't go anywhere." She stood up and walked out the door.

Becky waited for the door to close before she looked at Rodney. "Do you really think it's going to be that easy?"

"I don't know. I couldn't figure out why she wanted me to meet her to begin with. I'm still not sure I understand it. It was like she didn't think that I would believe her, but what was I going to do?"

"I don't know. It seems weird, but sometimes people do weird stuff, stuff where it's kinda hard to square with anything that resembles intelligence."

He couldn't argue with that. Stella didn't seem like she was the brightest bulb in the bunch. And Becky wondered what it was in her past that had caused her to become what she was. A bunch of bad decisions? The idea that she felt free whenever she was doing whatever she wanted, even if that was having sex with almost strangers? She wasn't sure. But she did know that wasn't the way to lasting happiness.

"We don't have to sit here and wait. There's a nice park across the street. We can take a walk."

"It's so nice to be without the babies. I miss them, but...we don't have heavy car seats to carry, and we don't have to worry about when they're going to eat next."

"It hasn't even been three weeks."

They grinned at each other. Becky had asked Vera if she would be willing to watch the babies for a day while they drove to Chicago to see the lawyer.

She hadn't said what it was about, although eventually it was going to come out that Rodney had a child. She figured she would let Rodney do that, whenever he wanted to, but she imagined that he would want to wait and see how it went today before he told everyone. Until the papers were signed, there was always a chance that Stella was going to back out.

"I guess I can't help but wish that there was some way we could help Stella too, you know?"

They had exited the lawyer's building and were waiting to cross the street to the park.

"Are you serious?" Rodney said, looking down at her. He seemed to be searching her face to see if there was any kind of guile or humor on it, but she was dead serious.

"Yeah." She nodded. "Doesn't it make you sad? I mean how misguided and pathetic she must be."

"Yeah. That's true. I...guess I can understand why you'd feel bad for her. I guess for me, I just want to stay away from her. I know she's bad news for me."

"She's still a temptation?" Becky asked, wondering for the first time if there was more there than what Rodney had said. After all, he'd avoided temptation all his life, except for with Stella. Maybe there was some kind of magnetic pull he had with her.

"No," he said immediately. "Not at all. It's more... I just know what kind of morals she has. And I know that I don't want to be caught in that same situation again. Where I'm alone with her. I don't think I would have any trouble resisting her. It's not that. It's just... I know she feels no guilt about what happened. And those kinds of people, people who don't see anything wrong with sleeping with anyone, are dangerous to married men and everyone." He held up his ring. "I really like being married, by the way."

She grinned. "It's funny, we're not getting any more sleep as a married couple than we did before we were married."

He laughed with her, knowing that was true. The twins had been up almost constantly every night of their marriage. It certainly had not been a romantic time for them.

"Maybe we can have Vera watch them overnight some night, so I might actually get to sleep with my wife. In the biblical sense," Rodney said, and then he laughed.

Becky figured it was okay. They had the rest of their lives. And she enjoyed some nice kissing before and after their nuptials. Considering that she was kinda new to the whole kissing thing, she was still greatly enjoying it too much to think she was missing anything else.

They walked around the park, holding hands and talking until Rodney dropped a bombshell on her.

"You know, I kinda thought your wedding gift would be here by now, but it was delayed a bit, and it's not going to be arriving until tomorrow."

"My wedding gift?" she asked, pulling her coat tighter around her as a cool wind blew off the lake.

"We can go back inside if you're cold?" Rodney said immediately.

"No thank you. I'm not cold, I just wanted to make sure the wind wasn't getting in any cracks." She turned to him. "Tell me more about this wedding gift?"

"Well, there's actually four of them. And I'm pretty sure you're going to be okay with it."

"I know it's not a refrigerator, and I sure hope it's not quadruplets.

Not that I would turn them down, but…I'm still getting used to the twins."

"No. Not quadruplets." He paused, maybe for effect. She almost prompted him again before he spoke. "I bought your Clydesdales back. It took me a little while to track them all down, but I had some help from the guy who hauled them away. I figured out who that was, called him, and it wasn't too hard for me to explain the situation and double the price on each of them. It was surprising how quickly they agreed to sell."

"Are you serious?" Becky laughed. It was a happy sound and carried across the park. Several people threw curious glances their way.

"I'm dead serious. They should be at our place tomorrow. You might want to, I don't know, order feed or something."

"Wow. And you have no idea how nice it's going to be to just pick up the phone and order feed and not have to count the pennies in my bank account first."

"You know, we never talked about that. I got the feeling, just different times when you were talking, that maybe things were a little tight for you."

Becky eyed him. Unsure whether she should admit just how bad they were. But there was no need for her to hide anything from him anymore. She trusted him completely. That didn't mean that he wasn't human and he wasn't going to make mistakes. She was too. But she wasn't going to hold him to some impossibly high standard. She was going to accept and forgive, and she was going to accept and forgive as often as it took. Because…that's what God did for her, and hopefully that's what Rodney would do for her as well. Why wouldn't she do it for him?

Maybe it would involve pain down the road. Maybe she would cause him pain too. And hopefully they would forgive and let it go and accept each other as they were. Broken, human, sinful, and love each other anyway.

"Yeah. They were pretty tight. I kept the heat turned down as low as it would go. I only had it on at all to keep the pipes from freezing. I wore layers and layers of clothes to bed, hoping to not freeze to death. I took a shower maybe once a week." She cringed. "Sorry. But it was too cold to take all of my clothes off, and the shower was kind of makeshift anyway. And I would have the heater on, and I really didn't have the money to pay for any extra heat. It was all I could do to buy feed for the horses. The day I sold them, I was out of feed and wasn't sure how I was going to buy any more."

"Wow. What were you eating?"

"Beans and rice. It was cheap, nutritious, but I don't care if I ever see beans and rice again. Sorry."

"It's okay. It's not my favorite either. Although you're right, it is nutritious." His mouth was set in a line. "I don't like to hear all that. It makes me feel even worse that I was so consumed with making more and more and more. And you needed me."

About that time, a car pulled up to the lawyer's office, and Stella got out.

She reached back in and soon stood with a little boy, holding him by the hand. He had dark hair and...dark skin.

"I don't think that one's yours," Becky said as they walked slowly out of the park and waited to cross the street.

Rodney huffed. "I don't think so either. I suppose that's probably why Stella wanted to meet with me. She didn't understand."

"Yeah. Wow."

"I suppose I'm supposed to feel like I've been duped, but I don't. I feel like we're getting a little boy out of this, who needed a good home, and I'm betting that because of the way the Lord works, we need this little boy in our lives."

"I bet you're right." Becky said, smiling up at him. She loved the way he thought. Loved that he wasn't angry at Stella for her lies and deceit, and loved that he wasn't determined to beat her at her own game. Because it was a game that involved lives and souls, and this little boy was more than just something to beat or something to win. He was someone who needed love.

Who needed them.

"Are you sure you're okay with this?" Rodney said, looking down at her.

"I am. I feel a little bit bad for you though. You confessed things to me that you didn't need to confess. And you paid money that you didn't need to pay. And I'm a little surprised you're not upset about that."

"Not at all. I would have told you anyway. I wouldn't have wanted that to be between us all of our lives. I wouldn't have felt right letting you think that I have been faithful all those years, even though I was ashamed. I wanted you to know the truth. Whether it was bad or ugly or what. And I don't feel the slightest bit angry. I just feel sad that Stella felt she had to lie and even worse that this little boy doesn't seem to have anyone who loves him."

"The five million dollars should have her set for life."

"I bet it won't though. That's why I'm having her sign release papers. I bet she goes through that in a year, maybe less."

"You're probably right," Becky said, figuring he knew.

"All right. Let's go do this. Let's go meet our son," Rodney said.

Becky nodded. There was a little boy in there who needed them and a woman who was struggling, who needed the Lord. Becky didn't know if she would have any words to say to her, but she would have a testimony to act out in front of her. And maybe, just maybe, Stella would see a little bit of Jesus in her. And it would change her life.

Twenty-Five

The morning sun filtered through the curtains as Becky slowly opened her eyes. For a moment, she reveled in the quiet that filled the bedroom—a peace made all the more valuable for its scarcity. With three kids under five in their home, life was hectic.

Rodney's arm was draped over her waist, his breathing steady against her neck. Being married to her best friend was better than she could have ever imagined. She smiled, still amazed at how quickly they had fallen into a comfortable rhythm as husband and wife. The road hadn't been entirely smooth, but each storm they weathered together had brought them even closer.

A small sound from the baby monitor drew her attention. Marley was stirring, though not yet demanding attention with her characteristic determination. Becky carefully extricated herself from Rodney's embrace and padded across the hardwood floor.

"I've got her," Rodney mumbled, his voice thick with sleep.

"Go back to sleep," she whispered. "I want to check on the horses anyway."

Rodney smiled without opening his eyes. "Tell Jasper good morning for me."

Jasper was his favorite, although Becky was not sure why. Still, she leaned down to kiss his forehead before slipping out of the room. The hallway was lined with three doors—two nurseries and one bedroom for Theo, Stella's son, whose legal adoption they had finalized just last month.

She peeked into Theo's room first. At nearly four years old, he had adjusted to his new life with remarkable resilience. There had been difficult nights, tantrums, and tearful questions about his mother, but he had slowly begun to trust them. Now he slept peacefully, clutching the stuffed horse Becky had given him when he first arrived.

In the nursery, Marley was awake but content, gnawing on her fist and kicking her legs. Kevin, predictably, remained asleep in his crib across the room.

"Good morning, sweet girl," Becky whispered, lifting Marley into her arms. "Want to come see the horses with me?"

After a quick diaper change and bundling Marley in a warm outfit suitable for the cool of early morning, Becky headed downstairs. She left a note for Rodney on the kitchen counter, though she'd already told him she was going to check the horses and she knew he wouldn't need a note to know where she'd gone.

Outside, the air was crisp but held the promise of warming into a beautiful Michigan summer day.

"Look, Marley," Becky pointed to the barn. "Where are we going?"

Marley babbled in response, her eyes wide as she took in the big building ahead of them. At seven months old, the twins were becoming more aware of their surroundings daily. It was fun to see their curiosity and enjoyment of the world around them.

As they approached the stable, familiar welcoming nickers reached her ears. The sound still brought tears to her eyes sometimes. When Rodney had surprised her by bringing her Clydesdales back, she had been overwhelmed with emotion. It had taken weeks to really believe they were hers again—that she could keep them without the constant worry of how to afford their care. She would always be grateful to Rodney for knowing her heart and wanting to give her everything, even though the longer she lived, the more she only wanted her family.

"Good morning, beautiful friends," she called as she entered the stable. Jasper's head immediately appeared over his stall door, his ears pricked forward in greeting.

"See the horsie, Marley?" Becky held her daughter up to see better, keeping a safe distance. Marley squealed and reached out her chubby hands.

"She's going to be just like her aunt," a deep voice said from behind her.

Becky turned to see Rodney standing in the doorway, Kevin in his arms.

"I thought I'd let you sleep," she said.

"And miss morning chores? Not a chance." He crossed to her side and kissed her softly. "Besides, this little guy decided he didn't want to miss out on the adventure."

Kevin gurgled happily, his eyes fixed on the massive horses.

"Where's Theo?" Becky asked.

"Still sleeping. I set up the monitor in the stable office so we'll hear when he wakes up."

This had become their morning routine when weather permitted— caring for the horses together while the children either joined them or stayed safely monitored in the house. It was different from the solitary mornings Becky had spent in her previous life, but so, so much better.

"I'm thinking of maybe offering a few days where I do carriage rides this summer," Becky said as she measured out grain. "Just weekend rides for tourists. Nothing too demanding."

Rodney smiled. "I think that sounds perfect. You know I'll help however I can."

"You're already doing more than I ever expected, running your business from home, helping with the kids."

"I wouldn't have it any other way," he replied, shifting Kevin to his other arm. "Though I admit, I'm glad I kept Angela as my assistant. She's been amazing at keeping everything organized while I'm changing diapers."

Becky laughed. "The great businessman, brought to his knees by tiny humans."

"The best kind of humbling." His expression grew more serious. "Any word from Stella?"

Becky shook her head. "Not since that postcard from Florida last month."

After the adoption, Stella had disappeared with her windfall. They received occasional postcards—Florida, Vegas, California—but no real communication. Becky had insisted they leave a door open, should Stella ever want to be part of Theo's life in a healthy way. Rodney had been skeptical but supportive of Becky's compassion.

"I've been praying for her," Rodney admitted. "I can't imagine living that way, always searching for the next thrill but never finding peace."

Becky nodded. "Me too, surprisingly. I will always have a place in my heart for her because she gave us Theo. And watching him bloom here with us—I can't help but be grateful."

As if on cue, the monitor crackled with sounds of Theo awakening. His sleepy voice called out, "Daddy? Mommy?"

The simple words still had the power to stop Becky's heart for a moment. The first time he had called her "Mommy" had been just weeks ago, and she treasured each instance.

"I'll go get him," Rodney said, handing Kevin to her. "He'll want to help with the horses."

As Rodney headed back to the house, Becky looked at the babies in her arms, then at the horses watching her expectantly. Her sister's absence was a constant ache, especially when she saw Rita's features reflected in the twins' faces. But there was joy too—a deep, abiding joy that came from the family God had created from broken pieces.

It wasn't the way she expected her life to turn out, but she couldn't have planned it better.

"Thank you, Lord," she whispered, "for all of this. For bringing us where we needed to be, even when the path wasn't what we expected."

Jasper nickered softly, as if in agreement. In the distance, she could see Rodney returning with Theo on his shoulders, the boy's laughter carrying across the morning air.

Six months ago, she couldn't have imagined this life. Now, she couldn't imagine any other.

"Becky?"

She turned at the familiar voice.

"Dad?" she said, unable to keep the shock out of her voice as she saw

Kristen and Luke striding up from where they'd parked by the barn. "You weren't supposed to be back for another month!" She recovered sufficiently to hurry toward them, a twin in each arm.

"Babies?" Kristen said, looking confused.

Becky had kept her promise to her sister. She hadn't told her parents anything that would have brought them home from Alaska early. Her heart sank as she thought about what she had to say. Rita's death being at the top. That would be hard, but there was Theo and Stella and Kevin and Marley. So many good things.

"Rodney and I have a lot to tell you."

Her dad's brows went up.

"It's mostly good," Rodney said, coming alongside of her, Theo's hand held safely in one of his, while he took Kevin so Becky could turn to her parents and throw her arms around them both.

"I missed you," she said as her mother held her close.

"And we missed you," Kristen said, sounding like she was fighting back tears. "All four of us just couldn't stay another day."

"Griff and Chi came back too?"

"They did. They were right behind us, but wanted to give us a few minutes with Becky." Luke looked at the kids again. "It seems like we've missed a lot."

"You have." Rodney met Becky's gaze. It wasn't going to be an easy conversation, but like the rest of the bumps in their marriage, they'd get through it and be closer for it. Plus, Luke and Kristen and Griff and Chi were going to be overjoyed about the kids.

The noise of tires on gravel made them all turn to see Griff and Chi pulling in.

"Let's go into the house. I can't wait to catch up." Becky smiled at her mom as she put her arm around Rodney's waist and they walked toward the house together. She said a silent prayer of thanks to the Lord, who had not withheld the cup of sorrow from her, but who had also filled her life with more love than she'd ever dreamed possible.

THANKS SO MUCH FOR READING! If you would like to stay in Raspberry Ridge just a little bit longer, I have great news! You can read about all the folks in town along with meeting a few new faces in the next book, Below the Far Horizon! You can order it HERE.

Continue reading for a sneak peek, and be sure to subscribe to my newsletter for updates and extra scenes HERE!

ENJOY THIS SNEAK peek of *Below the Far Horizon*:

Grace Tyack pulled into the driveway at her mother's house in Raspberry Ridge, the town in which she grew up, and pulled in a deep breath of cool, fresh, lake air.

Everything still looked the same. Large trees shaded the street that dead ended at the edge of a cliff, the base of which was surrounded by the Pebble Beach and that led to Lake Michigan.

The healing garden that was now at the end of the road, before the cliff, had been there when she'd been growing up, but that was one of the few changes.

A couple big houses on the hill she remembered from childhood look lived in and cheerful, rather than old and imposing the way she remembered them, but it could be her different perspective as an adult, rather than any specific changes that had been made.

Her mother's house was a block back from the dead end. Grace had been dreading the end of her trip, so she'd driven to the healing garden, sat there for a bit, and turned around.

She'd been tempted to park and walk through it, but she didn't want to meet anyone she knew.

She was saving all of her courage to face her mother.

It seemed the time had come.

Her sister, Stacy, would be there too.

Stacy and Mary Lou, her two sisters, one older one younger, had been taking care of their mother during her hip replacement from the beginning at the hospital with her and had gone through the first week of dealing with the aftermath of surgery and the hardest part of the pain.

They both needed to go back to their jobs, and Grace...Grace didn't have a job to go back to.

Taking another deep, cleansing breath, dreading the conversation she was going to have to have with all of her heart, Grace forced herself to touch the handle of the door before she yanked it and stepped out.

It was a BMW, and she owed too much on it to sell it and get out from underneath it. So she kept it, although she had no idea how she was going to pay the payments. She'd missed last month, and late notices were piling up in her mailbox.

That was one of the reasons she did not leave a forwarding address.

That, and while she knew her mother would be fine with her moving in permanently, her mother did not yet know that her husband had cheated on her and left, that the papers for her divorce were in the trunk of her car, and all she needed to do was sign them.

Her mother also didn't know that she was currently unemployed.

Yeah. Some success story she was. Her mother was sure to be proud.

Gritting her teeth and flexing her lips, practicing a smile that felt more like a snarl, she lifted her head, and put her shoulders back. She wasn't going to go slinking into the house. She had her pride after all. And, she'd left town, full of sass and confidence, sure that she was going to take the world by storm, beat it into submission, and come out on top.

That wasn't exactly what had happened.

Tulips bloomed along the wall, the same tulips that had come up every year of Grace's life. Red and purple and yellow and pink. Pretty and regal, the day they poked through the ground was always the day she finally felt she had evidence for the promise of spring.

Winters along the shores of Lake Michigan could be cold and

brutal. To put it mildly. Grace thought anyone and anything who could grow up and during those kinds of conditions would have to be strong and hardy.

But she hadn't exactly been strong and hardy as she fumbled and mumbled her way into the city, married the wrong man, got a job that she hated, and basically made a mess of her life.

Just the fact that you survived all of that means you are strong and hardy.

The voice spoke in her head as she put one foot on the porch step.

Really? Was it just the idea that she hadn't been brought to her knees, begging God for mercy that meant that she was stronger than she thought she was?

Or, maybe it was the idea that it wasn't her strength, but the Lord's. Because that was the one thing that the events of the last year had taught her. The religion of her childhood had a place in her life.

She continued on the steps, and then paused at the door. Should she knock?

She'd been back a couple of times for Christmas, staying only as long as necessary.

Her husband had come with her once, but the second time should come he'd insisted that he needed to stay and work, and couldn't take the time away from his job to accompany her to her home for Christmas.

She hadn't given him a hard time, because he hadn't been back to see his parents the entire time they'd been together. She'd never met them. She didn't even know if they really existed or if he'd hatched, or maybe been dropped out of an alien space craft, considering all the lies he told her over the years. Lies that hadn't come out until she figured out that he had been cheating on her, regularly, behind her back. His late nights of working had actually been meeting other women at bars. His work related expenses had been hotel bills, sure, but they were for the women that he'd hooked up with behind her back.

And she had been blissfully unaware.

What a farce her marriage had been. The one saving grace was the fact that her husband had adamantly refused her request to consider having children. She had begged and pleaded, wanting to start a family, buoyed by memories of her own family growing up beside the shores of Lake Michigan. They had been happy, idyllic days. Days she wanted to recapture, and maybe she thought the best way to do that would be to have a family of her own.

Still, her husband had adamantly refused. And, Grace had ended up being happy about that, after all of the details of his exploits had come out.

Maybe not of them. She actually did know if she knew all of them or not. Maybe there were things he had done behind her back that she had never found out about. That was quite possible. He wasn't exactly known as an honest person, or someone who ever told the truth. Ever.

She almost snorted. Her ex was the kind of person who didn't tell the truth if a lie would suffice.

The clean lake breeze lifted her hair. That part of her life was over now. She tried to push it out of her mind, and focus on the conversation she would be having when she stepped in the door.

Deciding a combination of knocking and walking in would be the best move, she rapped on the door before she opened it and stepped inside.

She had prepared herself for seeing her mother and the questions that her family would invariably ask. The confrontation of her sisters over the fact that she was broke, jobless, husbandless, and was driving a BMW that may or may not be repossessed in the near future. All of those things she expected, and felt she deserved, to be grown on.

What she hadn't expected was the way the scent of her mother's home, familiar and beloved and bringing back all of the happy and wishful memories of her youth, would hit her.

She was still reeling from the slightly yeasty smell, mixed with flowers and her mother's hand cream, when Stacy, her older sister, appeared in the doorway of the living room.

"I thought you were coming yesterday," Stacy said, in lieu of a greeting apparently.

Grace reminded herself that she needed to be humble. She'd been proud for way too long.

"I'm sorry. I...got held up." Not by anything in particular. Just by her own cowardice. She didn't want to leave her home, the home she lived in since she got married ten years prior. Her husband had claimed it had been a gift from his parents. Now she wondered. But, what else would it have been? His paramours hadn't exactly giving him money. It was the other way around.

Even though it had been a year since she first found out, pain still ball up inside of her. Maybe she was paying for all the lost dreams, or for the way that she had been determined to make a success of herself. To show everyone that even though she was a small town girl, she could play on the big stage.

And maybe it had to do with the fact that she was running from the memories, the tragedy that she never thought about, and that she wanted to overcome. To have so much success in her life that she never had to look back and think about what might have been. What she lost, what the people of this town lost.

"Mom is in the den. She prefers that room to this one, as you would know if you had been here at all."

"That's the way it was when we were little. I guess I remember."

Stacy gave her an eye. Maybe at the humility in her tone. Then she lifted her head in acknowledgment, turned around and started marching toward the den. Grace looked toward the kitchen, the bright cheerfulness still familiar and beckoning her, but she ignored the call. She needed to go see her mom. And Jill, her younger sister. Get those introductions and interrogations out of the way. If all three of them were in the room with her, perhaps she would only have to do this once.

Her mom sat on the couch, a soft blanket over her, wearing a comfy brown top, not jammies, although a worn pair of slippers sat beside the couch. They were not the slippers her mom had worn when she had been a child. Had those worn out? Been lost? Grace hadn't been around enough to know.

"Grace!" her mother said, looking up and holding her arms out.

Gita Honea was a naturally optimistic, happy person who'd made Grace's childhood idyllic. She'd been the perfect mother, as far as Grace could tell, even though Grace had gone through a period of rebellion in her teenage years, like every teenager again, right?

That wasn't true. She'd known teens who had grown closer to their parents during those years. Unfortunately, she didn't have that kind of wisdom at the time to know that was the best way for a person's life to go.

Now she did, but now was way too late. She wanted to apologize to her mother for the grief she caused during those years. But, this wasn't the time.

"Did you find out why she wasn't here yesterday?" Jill asked as she walked into the den behind them.

Stacy shook her head.

"I want a hug first," Gita said, continuing to hold out her arms.

Grace walked forward, embracing her mother, reveling in the familiar scent of vanilla and yeast and something sweet and dear to her heart.

It was the scent in this house that had turned her heart and stomach inside out.

That's what was going to make this next conversation more difficult, because the scent had brought back all of the love and laughter, and the tragedy too.

She straightened, her mother making sure to continue to grip her hands.

"I'm so glad you're here. I've missed you so much. I've only seen you a couple of times in the last decade."

That was a little bit of an underrepresentation of the truth. Grace had been here at least three times in the last ten years. And her mother had visited a handful of times in Indianapolis, where they'd settled.

Still, it hadn't been nearly enough. And Grace could honestly say, "I'm glad to be home."

She didn't think now is the time to tell her mother that she was broke, didn't have a job, and was hoping to move in with her. That would come later, after her sisters had left.

"I'm only able to stay until tomorrow. So you're going to have to learn everything that you need to do pretty quickly," Stacy spoke up. Always the one in charge. She was the perfect daughter. She lived just down the beach in Strawberry Sands, and she had the perfect family, a son and a daughter, a husband whose employer was in Chicago, although he worked from home three days a week.

Her life couldn't be any more perfect. She intimidated Grace, and perhaps Grace had spent so much time trying to be perfect, just so she could keep up with her sister.

"I have to leave tomorrow too. So it's going to be all on you, after that, Grace." Jill echoed her older sister's words.

Jill also had a perfect life, although she and her husband were childless. Still, they lived close, although further west and not right along lake. But she was a nurse at a local hospital and her husband was a doctor.

"You girls worry too much. Grace is perfectly capable of taking care of me, and she's completely cleared her calendar for the next six weeks, which is so generous and sweet of her." Her mother looked at her with so much admiration and love Grace could hardly stand it.

"You're worth it mom," she said, and tried to put some genuine feeling behind it, because she did believe it. But, she felt so guilty because the words her mom said weren't even close to being true. She had nowhere else to go. That's why she was here. Although, she would certainly help take care of her mom as she recovered. It would have just been a little bit more difficult to juggle her schedule.

"I'm going to show you a few things, and then Jill and I are going to go out for lunch. We've been here twenty-four/seven since we got here, and we deserve a little time off." Stacy spoke like it was a given, although somehow her words made Grace feel like she was being left out. Of course, she could have come two weeks ago, but the idea of being with her mom in the hospital, under all that pressure, and scared to death as to whether or not she would make it, and then all of the pain-and-suffering after she got out. She just couldn't stand the idea. And then, the papers had arrived, needing her signature.

That threw her for another loop and kept her away another week. The idea of confronting her sisters and admitting what her life was like was the reason she had delayed one more day.

She didn't want to delay anymore.

That wasn't true. She wanted to, but she wasn't going to allow herself to. Digging deep, she took a breath, and then met older, and most intimidating sister, right in the eye. "Stacy, if you wouldn't mind, I have something I need to tell all of you, and since we're all here, this is a good time."

Stacy blinked, like she couldn't believe that there was something in her sister's life that she didn't know about. Still, her sister's usually busy hands were quiet in front of her, and she waited, as though this were going to be a one sentence explanation and then she could get on with her life.

"I think you probably should sit down." Grace realized her voice sounded very timid. She tried to infuse confidence in it. "And mom, I'm sorry to do this to you when you're not feeling the best —"

Her mom waved a hand. "I feel fine. A little bit of pain occasionally, but the girls have been great at keeping up with the pill schedule, and I've been able to do all of my physical therapy, and I'm well ahead of the norm, which is what my therapist said."

She probably should ask after her mother's health and how the surgery went and all that. They'd been in touch via text and phone calls, but not nearly as much as her mother would have preferred.

"That's good. It sounds like you're going to be up and about in no time."

"I hope so. My craft supply is getting rather low. The girls have been great at mailing the things out, but you are the only one who was ever able to make anything even remotely similar to what I can."

Grace nodded, knowing what her mom said was true. She was the only one that had inherited their mom's artistic flair. The other two girls were way too serious and analytical to be able to do anything even remotely artistic. Still, they could package up the crafts as they were ordered online and ship them out, as their mom had just said. That didn't take any kind of artistic flair at all, except perhaps wrapping them.

"I'm feeling so well that I probably could start making things again, and I've had so much time to just sit and scroll through different social media and websites that my ideas are practically overflowing in my brain."

For the first time since she'd come, Grace felt a little trickle of excitement. She could help her mom out. She would be good at that. But, is that really what she wanted out of her life? To sit at home and make crafts and sell them online? Where was the prestige and that? She had wanted more out of her life, and people had expected more out of her.

She didn't want to let them down, but that was ironic, considering that she already had.

"Well?" Jill asked, perched on the edge of the imitation leather recliner that sat next to the couch.

Preview Chapter 2

Stacy had gracefully folded herself into a chair right beside her mother's feet, with a hand, gentle and comforting, on Gita's ankle.

"Well, I figured you guys were going to hear this eventually, probably sooner than later considering how small towns are." She hadn't had to worry about how small towns were for a really long time. That had been one of her considerations whenever she had decided to come. Her whole family was going to know exactly what happened.

She tried not to think about anything other than her story, not the nervousness that spun like sticky spider webs in her stomach, or the disappointment that was sure to be on her mother's face, and perhaps the gloating and I told you so look, that her sisters would have.

"I was fired from my job two months ago."

"No! I mean, you didn't really like that job, but you made good money," Stacy said immediately. And she looked truly distressed.

She was absolutely right on too. Which surprised Grace. Like Stacy had actually paid attention to her over the years, the few times they talked. Her job overseeing the various departments of the private university where she worked, had not been a job that she loved, but it had paid really well.

"At least your husband still has work," Jill said, and Grace assumed that was her way of trying to comfort her.

"Yes." Her fingers picked at the hem of her shirt. "Only he had multiple affairs, and I signed the divorce papers before I left Indianapolis. They're in the back of my car."

"You divorced?" her mother said, the comfort and concern in her tone almost making tears come to Grace's eyes.

"Yes. Were officially divorced. The judge just needs to file papers. I need to mail them to my lawyer. I didn't take the time to do that." She was supposed to have done it yesterday, which was ostensibly the reason that she stayed home, but she hadn't gotten out of bed except to go to the bathroom. Her shades were drawn and she'd spent the day crying. Thank goodness for eye drops, since it had taken an entire bottle to make her eyes presentable today.

"Oh my goodness. I didn't know there was any trouble at all," her mother said, pushing up with her elbows, before Stacy reached over and motioned for her to stay down. At first, Grace didn't think that Gita was going to listen, but she relaxed back into the couch after wincing.

"Yeah. I didn't want to bother anyone. It was...difficult." To say the least. She had built a life based on the two of them being to gather forever. She certainly hadn't expected anything to happen to him, and certainly had never even dreamed that he might cheat.

"So yeah, I'm jobless, divorced, and I'm behind on most of my bills. He hasn't been paying me, and up until I lost my job, there was no leg for me to stand on because I made as much as he did. I hardly think a judge is going to reverse that just because I got fired. Especially considering that happened almost a year after we separated."

Thankfully he had moved out, although it had taken her dipping into her savings to be able to make the mortgage on their condo by herself. They had definitely overextended on that. And then there was her car payment. She paid it, because she knew she was going to take it with her, but, after she lost her job, the severance package was just enough for her to pay her share of the lawyer fees for the divorce and the closing cost for the house. She had literally nothing.

"I'm so sorry to hear that. I thought you were doing fine." Jill stood up, and walked over, putting a hand on Grace's shoulder almost as though to check the temperature before she leaned down and gave her a warm hug.

Grace hadn't been sure what to expect from her sisters. They hadn't been especially close growing up. Although, she liked them both, and they talked some. Still, they'd drifted even further apart after they'd all gotten their own families, and Grace had made no effort to stay close.

She'd been busy trying to make her life a success, and she supposed also to make herself relevant compared to them.

The room was quiet for a bit, the silence feeling heavy and hard, before Stacy said, "What are you going to do?"

The question she dreaded. The unknown was always scary. "Well, right now I'm going to take care of mom. That's what I'm going to do for the next four weeks."

"And you're welcome to move in. You know you always have a home here."

She winced. "I don't really want to go backwards in my life." It was too late for that, but either the other ladies in the room didn't think that or they were too polite to say it, since no one said anything. She felt guilty at her mom's hurt look. "I'm sorry. I appreciate the offer, and I probably will stay a little bit if you don't mind. At least until I get back on my feet."

"Of course I don't mind!" Gita said, smiling with all the love and affection in her mother's heart at her. It made her own heart tremble and want to cry.

But she was not allowing herself the luxury of tears. Not today. That was yesterday, when she signed the papers and mailed them. And realize that that part of her life was truly over. Her husband wasn't going to apologize and come back. They weren't going to attempt to sweep the ashes away and rebuild. There was no going back. It was only going forward, in a direction she hadn't anticipated, with one foot in front of the other, as painful and hard as that was.

"If there's anything I can to help, you know I will. Tony might be able to put a word in for you at his job in Chicago if you'd like." Stacy always was a fix-it kind of person. "Or I can see if the company where I work is hiring. I haven't been paying attention, since I just do my job, and spend as much time with my children as I can. You don't get this time of their lives back."

Grace nodded, although she was so far from thinking about things like that it seemed like Stacy was talking about another time and place.

"The hospital might be hiring in the administrative section. You've got plenty of experience. I can check and see and get you the information if you'd like," Jill said, and her tone was sweet and helpful.

Maybe it would be easier if her sisters had been gloating and laughing at her. Telling her that she had left with such fanfare, so prideful and arrogant, so certain she was going to take the world by the tail and slap it to the ground, reminding her of how much she thought of herself, and how wrong she was.

But they hadn't, and their kindness and forgiveness of her arrogance and inconsideration was almost more than Grace could stand.

And neither of them had mentioned what she had done to Claire.

Those were all memories that belonged to yesteryear, or that's what she told herself. Although she knew with coming back to a small town, she would probably have to face them, perhaps on a daily basis for who knew how long, since small towns never forgot anything.

"You two go on. It's lunchtime for you, and I'd like to talk to Grace myself. I've not had a chance to for so such a long time and surely there are some good things that I've missed," Gita said, making a shooing motion toward Grace's sisters.

They reluctantly got up, with both of them talking about the different things that they did to help their mom. Stacy showed the pain med schedule and made sure Grace knew when the next pill was supposed to be given.

"We've been keeping her on a very strict schedule. The physical therapist said that was probably the main reason why she was doing so well. Because her pain has been managed."

Grace nodded, thinking that she'd managed to screw up everything else in her life, she would hate to screw this up too. But obviously Stacy didn't have a whole lot of faith in her ability to be able to do a good job. Either that, or she was just being Stacy, who had to control everything.

Grace figured it was probably more the latter, but it felt more like the former. That's how she felt about herself. There was no grace for the mistakes that she'd made, or the problems that she brought on herself.

It wasn't too long until her sisters left, and Grace was left sitting alone beside her mother, wondering if her mom really wanted to talk to her, or was just trying to shoo her other daughters out so they could take a much needed break.

"I'm sorry you had to come back in such terrible circumstances. I have to admit I'm a little hurt that you didn't talk to me at all," Gita said, adjusting herself to a more comfortable position.

Grace sat for just a moment, just soaking in the feeling of someone caring. Why had she not wanted to come home? But then realized she was the one who was supposed to be taking care of her mother. She got up and fluffed the pillows, tucking one closer down into her lower back.

"How's that?" she asked.

"Are you avoiding my comment?" Gita said, before she said, "That's just fine."

"I suppose I am." She forced her throat to work. "Mom. I'm sorry. I guess I was just so... Driven to show everyone that I could be successful. And by successful I mean money and houses and cars and stupid stuff that doesn't matter now. Because I lost it all. It doesn't matter how successful you are; it can all come crashing down."

"I'm surprised that Lonnie turned out to be such a terrible cheater. I wouldn't have guessed."

Her mom truly sounded distressed.

"I know you didn't know him very well when we got married. But I thought I did. I thought we would be together forever." She didn't know what else to say, and she shrugged her shoulders, lifting her hands, indicating that she didn't have the words. "I guess that's what everyone thinks on their wedding day."

"I don't know about anyone. But that's what I thought, too. It's hard to imagine someone cheating after saying vows in front of God."

"There's so much temptation from so many different directions. So many ways you can see other people who are cheating and enjoying it and trying to convince you that it's not that bad."

"I was concerned when you got married so young."

She had been twenty-two and hadn't graduated from college. All of her friends had slept around and weren't in a huge rush to get married. They had said exactly what her mom said, that they didn't want to get married young, but she and Lonnie were trying to live what they believed. Grace could roll her eyes over that, since she hadn't lived what she believed in any other area. She'd been so desperate for money and prestige and all the trappings of showing everyone how she'd become successful in the world's eyes, that she lost sight of the things that really mattered.

"I don't think it's the age I got married. We didn't fornicate before we were married like so many of my friends. I didn't want to go that route, and Lonnie agreed." Looking back, she wondered if he had agreed, or if he had just been happy he found someone gullible enough to marry him. Or, maybe he'd just been placating her, and figured a wife would be a good cover for his escapades.

She'd already been through all that. The idea that he couldn't possibly have been pure like he had claimed on their wedding night, and wondering how many women he'd been with before her, and how many he'd been with during their marriage. The idea made her sick to her stomach, and she had to shove it aside. She'd spent more than enough time thinking about that, and she didn't want to have those thoughts in her head anymore at all.

"I admire that. I think you have that part right," her mom said firmly, as though she needed to reassure Grace of something.

"Thanks. I had so many other parts wrong."

"All the things that you had wrong are things that you now know are wrong, so you can learn from them."

Her mom was a big believer in positive thinking and in turning trials into steppingstones. Grace had heard that all her life. Maybe her mom was right, but sometimes a person just wanted to wallow.

Of course, wallowing wasn't a good idea. One could really spiral downward quickly.

"I think you're right mom. I need to do that. I just haven't figured out how." That was a problem. How did she make those things magically become the steppingstone she used to turn her life around and become...better?

"I think you've done the right thing. You're here and there is no pressure, although you've always been very good at crafts and artsy things, and you've loved doing them, too. Plus, I need help. I didn't tell this to the girls, but I had trouble keeping up with the latest trends. I... I guess I'm a little burned out. Or maybe lonely. I'm not sure."

Grace blinked. "Mom. I didn't know."

Her mom waved a hand as though it were nothing. "I didn't want to burden anyone. Probably like you," she said with a little smile. "But you girls have been gone for so long, and it's just day in day out, more of the same. I'm tired. Maybe it was a little bit of the pain of my hip, but I just lost my spark for life."

Kristin didn't know what to say. Her mom was always that happy and energetic and the kind of person who always found the positive no matter how hard it was. To hear this shocked her.

"Mom. You are the most positive person I know. I can't believe you're saying this." Did her mom need a change of scenery? Was she saying she wanted to move? Michigan winters could be brutal.

"Maybe you just need to get on a dating site and find someone."

Her mother laughed. "Maybe. I tried a couple of sites, but it's so easy to lie. I've been tempted to lie. And I'm not normally a liar. I don't know how I could trust anyone to tell the truth on those things, you know?"

Her mom was right. It was always best to have someone helping to sort truth from fiction. "You shouldn't have done that without someone knowing. Did you tell Stacy or Jill?"

"I haven't told anyone."

"You could meet a serial killer. Someone should be watching out for your welfare."

"I'm glad you're concerned. But nothing is happening, because I haven't responded to anyone. I actually took my profile down a while ago, it just...I told the Lord that if I was to get married again, I was going to have to meet the man in person, because this online stuff is just too untrustworthy."

Her mother was smart.

Grace had been duped by a man who was obviously untrustworthy, and it hadn't even occurred to her to be concerned about him lying. She just...believed Lonnie. Everything he said, she took it as gospel truth. She was such a fool.

"I'm glad to hear that mom. But not happy about the others. You are lonely. And, it sounds like you're depressed."

"I wouldn't go so far as to say I'm depressed, but I have been struggling. The idea that you might come live with me has perked me up like nothing has in a long time."

Was her mother just saying that? Did she want to take away any stigma or guilt or shame that she felt for moving backwards in her life? After all, what thirtysomething wanted to move back in with her mother? Unless, of course, their mother needed them. And then, she would move heaven and earth to help her.

Neither one of her sisters could. They were both happily married with jobs and homes of their own. They couldn't move back in, but she could.

"Are you serious about that?"

"I am. I wasn't going to tell you any of my problems. I didn't want to burden you. But, when you came and said that you didn't have anywhere else to go, it gave me hope that I haven't felt in a long time." Her mother paused. "But of course, if you find something else that makes you happy, don't feel like you have to stay with me. I'm not in that kind of situation."

"No. I know," Grace said, and she knew exactly what her mother was saying. Her mother would prefer, every day all day long, that Grace be happy. Her mother certainly would never want her living with her, if Grace would prefer to do something else.

Gita was such a great example of selflessness, and someone who lived to be a blessing to others.

"You think about it. You don't have to do anything. And you know I'll help you with whatever you decide, and as long as you're doing right, I'll support you however I can."

"I know mom. I'm sorry that I haven't been back in so long. I feel guilty about that." She felt guilty for a lot of things, stemming back long before she got married.

"Don't feel guilty. You can look back, learn from your mistakes, but don't let guilt drag you down. It will ruin your life. And you end up wasting it, instead of using it in the best way possible."

Grace nodded, knowing her mother was right.

"Now, if you don't mind, I'm going to take a little rest. The girls seem to think that they need to hover over me every second of every day, but I'm able to get up and down now without any assistance. And the only thing I needed them for was if I would fall for some reason, I might not be able to get up on my own."

"I definitely wouldn't want that to happen," Grace said.

Gita nodded. "I promise I will not try to get up if you're not here. Now, why don't you go take a rest, or maybe you can take a walk. The healing garden at the end of the road is a great place to go to try to gather your thoughts. Or you could go take a walk along the beach."

"Are you sure?"

"I am. Physical therapy comes in two hours. So, you really don't need to be back for at least three."

"All right. Although, I think I probably ought to be here when physical therapy is here, so I can see what exercises you're supposed to be doing."

"Oh trust me, Stacy's got that covered," her mom said, with a slight amount of sarcasm in her voice.

Grace and Gita shared a smile over Stacy's controlling nature. Just because someone wasn't perfect didn't mean a person couldn't love them anyway. Her mother had said that to her a million times, if she'd said it once.

"I think I will take a short walk, but I'll be back long before physical therapy gets here."

Her mother nodded, settling down amongst the pillows while Grace adjusted them.

"I'm sorry about everything that's happened. But I'm glad you're home." She smiled, as she shifted slightly and closed her eyes.

Grace had to agree. She, too, was glad she was home.

Sign up for Jessie's newsletter! Get a free book, access to exclusive bonus content, get fun and funny updates on her life on the farm and more!

Sign up for Jessie's newsletter! Get a free book, access to exclusive bonus content, get fun and funny updates on her life on the farm and more!

A Gift from Jessie

View this code through your smart phone camera to be taken to a page where you can download a FREE ebook when you sign up to get updates from Jessie Gussman! Find out why people say, "Jessie's is the only newsletter I open and read" and "You make my day brighter. Love, love, love reading your newsletters. I don't know where you find time to write books. You are so busy living life. A true blessing." and "I know from now on that I can't be drinking my morning coffee while reading your newsletter – I laughed so hard I sprayed it out all over the table!"

Claim your free book from Jessie!